A Gruesome End

John hoped that Montoya was on his way back to the ranch, and he kept that hope until they rounded a bend in the road and saw the wagon, canted slightly with one wheel in a ditch, the horses standing forlorn and hipshot.

John felt something squeeze his heart, an intangible and disembodied pressure that stopped his breath for just a second or two.

Flies zizzed around in aimless circles above the wagon bed, their bodies glinting sparkles of blue and green. The horses switched their tails and made little whispers that were as ominous as any John had ever heard.

Like whispers in an outdoor mausoleum.

He rode alongside the wagon, his teeth clamped tight, his jaw rigid, as if he was about to face a nightmare in the golden haze of daylight. The muscles in his stomach tautened as his mind braced him for shock. He looked into the wagon bed, and there, amid the sacks of flour, sugar, and beans, the cans of coffee, and the sacks of oats and corn, Montoya lay sprawled like a broken scarecrow, his eyes glassed over with the frost of death, staring up at a blue sky clotted with clouds, and a hideous grin across his throat, gaping like a clown's mask, flies nipping at the dried blood, the sizzling sounds of their wings assaulting John's ears with the indecency of their hunger.

"I found Montoya."

Savage Vengeance

Jory Sherman

BERKLEY BOOKS, NEW YORK

THE BERKLEY PUBLISHING GROUP
Published by the Penguin Group
Penguin Group (USA) Inc.
375 Hudson Street, New York, New York 10014, USA

Penguin Group (Canada), 90 Eglinton Avenue East, Suite 700, Toronto, Ontario M4P 2Y3, Canada
(a division of Pearson Penguin Canada Inc.)
Penguin Books Ltd., 80 Strand, London WC2R 0RL, England
Penguin Group Ireland, 25 St. Stephen's Green, Dublin 2, Ireland (a division of Penguin Books Ltd.)
Penguin Group (Australia), 250 Camberwell Road, Camberwell, Victoria 3124, Australia
(a division of Pearson Australia Group Pty. Ltd.)
Penguin Books India Pvt. Ltd., 11 Community Centre, Panchsheel Park, New Delhi—110 017, India
Penguin Group (NZ), 67 Apollo Drive, Rosedale, North Shore 0632, New Zealand
(a division of Pearson New Zealand Ltd.)
Penguin Books (South Africa) (Pty.) Ltd., 24 Sturdee Avenue, Rosebank, Johannesburg 2196,
South Africa

Penguin Books Ltd., Registered Offices: 80 Strand, London WC2R 0RL, England

This is a work of fiction. Names, characters, places, and incidents either are the product of the author's imagination or are used fictitiously, and any resemblance to actual persons, living or dead, business establishments, events, or locales is entirely coincidental. The publisher does not have any control over and does not assume any responsibility for author or third-party websites or their content.

SAVAGE VENGEANCE

A Berkley Book / published by arrangement with the author

PRINTING HISTORY
Berkley edition / July 2011

ISBN: 978-0-425-24207-0

BERKLEY®
Berkley Books are published by The Berkley Publishing Group,
a division of Penguin Group (USA) Inc.,
375 Hudson Street, New York, New York 10014.
BERKLEY® is a registered trademark of Penguin Group (USA) Inc.
The "B" design is a trademark of Penguin Group (USA) Inc.

PRINTED IN THE UNITED STATES OF AMERICA

10 9 8 7 6 5 4 3 2 1

For Lou Turner and Squeak

1

JOHN SAVAGE SAT ON THE PORCH OF HIS EMPTY CABIN. HE SIPPED his coffee, the aroma of Arbuckles cinnamon stick long gone. He could almost taste the tin in the battered cup that had once been his father's favorite when he was alive and they had worked the creek, panning for gold. The steam rose up over the rim as he tipped the cup to his lips. He felt the warm mist seep into his eyes like tears from another time, another place.

He stared up at the stars in the paling sky. It seemed to him that they had all moved at once, leaving silver streaks across his retinas, and the vapor made them blur into melted diamonds until, putting the cup down, his eyes cleared. He set his cup next to the chair Emmalene had left behind because she knew he liked to sit in it of an evening when they would talk and watch the sunset turn the high clouds to ash as it sank behind the snowcapped peaks. The mist didn't go away, and he realized that his eyes had filled unexpectedly with tears. Just to think of Emma gone, though it had only been about three days, made him sentimental and sad. He had grown fond of the woman and her daughter, Evangeline. They had become squatters on his land, unwittingly, when Argus Blanchett had brought them there—Emma's husband, Eva's father. And John had killed Argus down in Cherry Creek, without knowing who he was, only that he was a bad man who had tried to kill him.

Emma—he had begun calling her that as he had come to know her better—was still mourning the death of her son, Whit. Bad like his pa, Whit had taken his own life. Eva had taken Whit's death even harder than her mother. Yet the young woman was nothing like her brother. *Nothing like her father, either,* he thought. But he granted that this place held worrisome memories for both Emma and Eva. Whit was buried on a little knoll in the pines, just a few yards off from his grazing land, away from the cattle, deep in the ground where the wolves and the coyotes could not get at him.

He had become fond of Emma, and he thought they might have been able to get past the sadness, the grief, and that cloud of death that hung between them like some nameless phantasm. She was a comely woman, with her auburn hair, her alabaster skin, her dimpled chin. Then, below his and Ben's claim, another party of men had found color in their pans and the hard-rock miners had come in and found veins of gold in the bluffs above the creek.

Other men had come, and they had built a small town just a few miles from John's claim, hauling in lumber and building log cabins, putting in stores and a little bank, a church, even a weekly newspaper that boasted the progress of the town and the miners who hauled ore down to Denver, built *arrastres*, and brought in mules. They made whiskey and beer and opened a tavern at one end of town and then another at the other end. One day, a man rode up and of-fered both Emma and Eva jobs at his mercantile store. Emma washed clothes and Eva ironed them, and they had moved away to a new house in the town they were calling Butterfly Creek because, when the first prospectors came to pan gold, hundreds of yellow-winged butterflies hatched from their brown cocoons, and the men took it as a sign that there was gold in the water and in the limestone bluffs that shone golden in the morning sun.

The good part of it was that the restaurant owners bought his beef and drove the cattle to the slaughterhouse at no expense to him. Otherwise, it was an unwelcome settlement in a wilderness he had come to love. The settlers had brought all the sins of civilization with them and taken away Emmalene and Evangeline to wash their filthy clothes and sell dry goods at exorbitant prices.

He heard the gentle lowing of the cattle as they stirred in their Stygian pools of shadows, sounding like lost souls moaning in some nocturnal Hades. The smell of them and their offal drifted to his nostrils, mingling with the scent of columbines and the faint musk of morning glories, their petals still folded in green cocoons, flowers Emma had planted in beds bordering his porch. And the agony of those aromas made his innards twist into rippling knots as if her hands were twisting his muscles into three-ply ropes slick with his own coursing blood.

He had never spoken to her of his feelings for her. He had never told her that when she came near or touched him, his heart raced and pounded like an Arapaho tom-tom. Nor did she know what her smile did to him, melting some hard, bitter something inside him until his vocal chords seized up with the hot wax of desire. And when she touched him, his loins burned from the glow of her hand and his manhood fattened in the white cradle of his underwear.

He felt the surge of unbidden tears and snatched his pistol from its holster. The pistol his daddy had left him, a beautiful Colt .45 that he had modified to suit a boy who would become a man. He gripped it hard and squeezed the tears with his eyelids, his throat turning raw and sore and dry as withered corn husks. He looked down at the faint gleam of the legend his father had engraved on the blued barrel, the words illegible in the darkness but seared into his brain with its quicksilver scroll.

No me saques sin razón,
Ni me guardes sin honor.

The liquid Spanish translated to: *Do not draw me without reason, nor keep me without honor.*

It's the damned gun, he thought. *That's what drove Emma away from me.*

The savage gun. The same gun that had killed Emma's husband. And so many others, bad men all.

But he who lives by the gun shall die by the gun crawled across the velvet escarpment of his mind, like some warning serpent flushed from an ebony garden.

The damned gun. The cursed gun.

He brought the pistol up, turning his hand so that he could peer at its steel snout and think about the deaths it had issued from its metal throat, the men it had killed and the men it might yet kill. He thought of the woman it may have driven away under the hypnotic spell of its deadly curse.

"Damned gun," he cried out and toyed with the thought of cocking it and slipping his finger inside the guard and squeezing that hair trigger just once, just enough to blot out all pain and erase all memory in a single explosive roar that would echo up the valleys of the mountains and make the cattle jump and run like rabbits through the high grasses of spring.

He heard the crunch of boots and dropped the gun to his side.

A figure loomed out of the darkness and approached the porch.

"You got a problem with your gun, Johnny?"

"Ben, you got more mouth than brains," John said.

"I smelt coffee. You got any to spare?"

Ben Russell came up on the porch, his bearded face in shadow, his bulk making the boards creak and whine under his boots.

"I used the last of it, but there's another cup or two in the pot."

"Out of coffee and everything else, I reckon."

"Carlos brought all that stuff up last night, didn't he?"

"That's just it, John. Ain't seen hide ner hair of Carlos. Wagon ain't in the shed. Let me get some coffee in this growlin' belly and we'll talk."

Ben went into the cabin. John holstered his pistol and watched the sky pale to the east. A thin line of cream defined the horizon. A pale blue sky washed the stars away as dawn crept up the firmament pushing the black away with the soft color of a robin's egg. He heard Ben banging the cups in the cupboard, the clank of the coffeepot as he set it back on the woodstove, his heavy footsteps as he walked back toward the front porch.

Carlos Montoya had hauled the last of Emma's furniture down into town. He was supposed to buy coffee, flour, beans, bacon, sugar, and such and haul them back to the ranch. He should have arrived shortly after nightfall.

Ben sat down on a rough-hewn bench next to the wall.

"I looked for Carlos, waited up for him," Ben said, blowing on his coffee. "Finally went to bed."

"I wasn't even thinking about him," John said.

"You ain't slept a dadgummed wink, have you, Johnny?"

"I catnapped some. Wasn't listening for that wagon, I guess."

Ben drank a sip of coffee and rolled it around in his mouth before he swallowed the liquid. John could hear it swish in his mouth.

"Reckon Carlos got tied up in one of them cantinas?" Ben said.

"Not Carlos. He doesn't drink and he doesn't dance."

"Maybe he run into a Mex friend."

John finished his coffee and stood up. He could see the cattle now, and his gaze swept the expanse of grassland, the blades still in shadow, the sun still buried in the east but gilding the far clouds and stitching the gray cotton with orange and rosy sprays, a slight tinge of silver that shimmered along the lower edges.

"Who's riding night herd?" John asked.

"Ah, lemme see. Juanito took over at dusk. On till midnight. Should be . . . nope, Gasparo took that shift. Juanito is ridin' herd till sunup. Should be headin' back to the bunkhouse by now."

Ben looked off to his right at the cluster of buildings, empty hitchrails, the barn.

John glanced that way, too.

"Nope. Ain't back yet."

"There's nobody watching the herd, Ben," John said, and his voice was leaden, weighted with the worry that was a hand pressing hard on the back of his neck.

He felt the silence rush up to him as the blazing orange rim of the sun scoured the cream rent in the sky and pierced the clouds with its rays expanding like a giant Japanese fan.

"Something's wrong," John said, his voice barely above a whisper. "Something's damned wrong."

"Hell, ain't no need—" Ben Russell started to say. His thought and his voice were shut off by the piercing scream that shot across the pasture from the fringe of the pines bordering the grassy sward.

Both men stiffened. Ben set his cup down on the bench and stood up.

The second scream was filled with blood and terror. It was much louder than before. It was full of agony and desperation.

And it made the hackles on the back of John's neck stiffen and crawl with icy lice that streamed down his back with tiny racing claws.

Ben cursed.

John missed all the steps and hit the ground running. Ben clambered off the porch right behind him, his shirttail slipping out of his trousers and flapping against his butt like a tattered battle flag whipped by the winds of exploding cannons.

2

THERE WAS ONE MORE SCREAM.

This one ripped through John's eardrums and screeched in his brain like human flesh being torn apart by some savage beast. It was a scream that embedded itself in his brain as if a hot coal had been plunged into his lungs and gut. It burned a permanent memory deep in the recesses of his mind.

And midway through the long ribbon of the man's scream, it was cut short, as if someone had sliced the ribbon of sound in two with a terrible swift sword.

There were no dying notes in the scream. It just shut off, leaving a silence that was like a hundred kettle drums pounding in John's ears.

As he ran, it seemed the world had become a vacuum, that something had sucked all the air out of his lungs and the meadow and the caverns of his ears. It was as if some part of him had gone deaf while another throbbed at his temples like a gandy dancer's ten-pound maul.

A pair of heifers bolted away from John as he ran toward them. He dodged a steer as he headed for the timber, running through the wet grass that made a swishing sound against his trouser legs. His boots thudded on the earth, his heels barely touching as he dashed forward on the balls of his feet. Light seeped onto the meadow with the pale fingers of dawn pushing the shadows toward the snowcapped mountains, the dark ranch buildings standing silent at the far end of the pasture.

He was vaguely aware of Ben running behind him, thrashing through the grass with a swish-swish sound and the rhythmic thumping of his boots ticking like a grandfather clock in John's eardrums.

He entered the timber at an angle where the darkness lingered in the pines and visibility was challenged. He stopped suddenly and hunched down, listening. He slid his pistol from its holster but did not cock it. He froze there, peering ahead of him and sweeping his gaze in a wide arc, looking for the slightest movement, any shape that should not be there, any sign of life or death.

Veils of pale golden light streamed through the gaps between the trunks of trees, gilding the fallen pine needles, shimmering with a silent electricity that John could almost feel against his eyes. Ben came up behind him, and John sensed that Russell was going to ask him a question. He turned and, with his left hand, put a finger to his lips. Ben nodded and drew his own pistol. The sound from the holster was like the soft slithering of a snake, and it was the only sound for a long moment when all creatures freeze into motionless statues and even the trees seem to hold their breaths.

Then there was a scurrying sound off to John's left and he saw the flash of a chipmunk, the nervous flicker of its tail, the rattle of tiny claws on vagrant stones scattered like a child's marbles among the fallen pinecones that looked like grenades left behind from a forgotten war.

More silence surrounded the two men as they turned their heads to listen for any slight sound.

They waited.

Waited for the unknown, for the great mystery of the scream to be revealed. Waited for the cough of a cougar, the grunt of a feeding lion.

They heard it then. Heard something. The crack of a dry branch, the muffled shuffle of a horse's hooves in the distance. It was a ghostly sound, a disembodied sound that made no sense to either man. It was too far away and might have been the noise of Juanito's horse running away, running away from its dead master. Or it might have been the retreating sound of a man riding away from the cutoff scream, the man who had caused the pain and the agonized shrieks and sliced them off with a long sharp blade.

"What do you make of it?" Ben whispered, leaning down so that his mouth was close to John's ear.

John shook his head.

The sound of the galloping horse faded away, faded into that deep hush of the forest at dawning until it was as if there had never been a sound at all, only imagination in the minds of Ben and John as they waited and listened for some sign of revelation, a clue to a terrible discovery just beyond earshot and the piercing gazes of their eyes.

John stood up and tiptoed over the brown rungs of pine needles, heading for that place where he figured the screams had rent the dawn only moments before. Ben followed him, his steps just as careful, just as mannered as a man walking through a dark hallway in a deserted fortress or an abandoned cathedral. They stepped through quavering shafts of feeble sunlight, deeper into the pines, through tall statues of brown wood and needled boughs, past the regal spruces and a bristling juniper tree, into a clearing where the horror was, where some of the answers were.

There, against a tree, was a hog-tied calf, its neck twisted so that its head stuck up at an impossible angle. Its eyes were glass balls of polished ebony; its pink-and-black tongue lolled out of its mouth, gripped by clamped teeth that shone like a hideous ivory grin frozen by rictus.

Someone, some vicious sonofabitch had broken the calf's neck with a sudden, violent wrench. Beyond the calf lay the body of the young Mexican, Juanito Alvarez, his throat cut to a wide, blood-drenched grin. John stepped over him and saw that the knife used to cut his throat had nearly decapitated him. He felt a sickness boil up out of his stomach. Bile surged up his throat, and he had to turn away and gulp deep drafts of air to keep from vomiting his morning coffee.

"Good lord," Ben breathed as he looked at the calf and the limp body of Juanito. The young man looked like a rag doll tossed on a bed of pine needles, his eyes and mouth painted on a bronze mask.

John stood up, held a hand to his stomach. He slid his pistol back in its holster and looked up through the trees at the blue sky like a rotunda dome—calm and serene as an ocean in the doldrums.

He turned and looked down at Juanito as Ben doubled over and spewed vomit from his mouth in a green-and-yellow spray that mottled the ground with bits of buttery corn, black beans, and scraps of half-digested bread. He croaked like some gawky seabird screeching over its decimated nest.

Ben uttered an oath amid his slobber and retched again, his eyes watering, the muscles in his neck quivering until the veins surfaced and turned a pallid purple.

"Poor Juanito," Ben said as he coughed. "He didn't deserve this. No way."

John saw something protruding from Juanito's woolen shirt, just beneath his sheepskin jacket. It looked like a brownish scrap of butcher paper, caught between two buttons.

"You see what happened here, Ben," John said. He walked over to Juanito's corpse and bent down to retrieve the scrap of paper. There was writing on it, words scrawled with a lead pencil.

"Looks like someone roped that calf and used it for bait."

"Yeah. Juanito heard a calf in trouble and rode in here to help it. Somebody jumped him and pulled him from his horse."

"What you got there, Johnny?" Ben wiped his mouth on his shirtsleeve.

"Looks like whoever murdered Juanito left us a note."

"What's it say?"

Ben peered over John's shoulder at the note.

John stepped from the shade of the pine tree and held the note in a thin beam of sunlight.

"It says: *See how easy it is, Savage? You stay away from Emmalene, you bastard. Stay plumb away or this is your fate.*"

"Huh?" Ben gasped.

John handed him the note.

"Here, you read it, Ben. I'm going to be sick, I think."

John walked away, leaned against a tree. Ben holstered his pistol and read the note, holding it close to his face and squinting at the cursive lettering.

"This don't make no sense. Emma's done moved to town and this bastard comes up here and murders poor Juanito. Whoever wrote this here note is plumb loco, you ask me."

John drew air into his lungs, fighting against the urge to throw up whatever was roiling in his stomach. His throat was constricted, his vocal chords taut with the strain of holding back both tears and the contents of his sandpapered stomach.

Both men heard a soft nicker coming from a few yards away. They both looked toward the sound and heard the pad of a horse coming their way.

The horse wove its way through the pines and approached them. It tossed its head and whickered gently when it saw the two men. Then it looked at the body of Juanito and stopped. It pawed the ground with a single hoof and drooped its head.

"That's Juan's horse," Ben said. "At least that bastard didn't kill Cholo."

The horse was a mottled gray, and Juanito had given it that name when he sold his wagon and bought Cholo in Denver so that he could go to work for John Savage.

"Catch Cholo up, Ben," John said. "We still have another problem."

"Eh? What's that?" Ben asked as he stepped toward the horse hanging its head low in a forlorn demonstration of its grief.

"Where in hell is Carlos Montoya and our supply wagon?"

Ben grabbed up Cholo's reins and stood stock-still, a look of sudden bewilderment on his face. His neck wattles, rimed with dirt and sweat, quivered as he swallowed saliva down a dry throat.

John's words hung in the air like some lost echo blown up an empty canyon where all echoes died in one final whisper.

3

THE MORNING POURED IN ON BEN AND JOHN AS THEY HEFTED
Juanito's body onto the saddle. John cut the rope around the
calf's legs and tied Juanito's hands and feet together loosely,
looping the rope around the saddle horn and through the
stirrups.

"If I forget, Ben," John said, "tell Gasparo, or someone,
to butcher that calf. No use in wasting the meat."

"I can do it, John."

"We're going to look for Montoya and that wagon as
soon as I saddle up Gent."

"You want me to go along?"

"Two heads are better than one," John said as they walked
through sunbeams and shadows, away from that place of
death. Ben held Cholo's reins while John took the lead.
"Even if one of them is always thinking of grub."

"Aw, Johnny, that ain't fair. I was just thinkin' of the sun
swellin' up that dead calf fore I could skin it out."

"I know," John said in a kindly tone. He was already thinking of something else.

A few of the cattle moaned and moved out of their way as they walked across the sunstruck pasture, beadlets of dew sparkling like jewels, a meadowlark trilling a lyrical arpeggio off by one of the creeks. A mountain quail piped up from somewhere along the fringe of pines on the opposite side of a pasture, and the first hawk of the day cleared the treetops behind John's cabin, shifting its wings so that it drifted on silent pinions toward the meadowlark's position.

John loved this country, the wildness of it, and now someone was trying to spoil it again, just like Ollie Hobart, who had murdered John Savage's entire family and a lot of innocent, hardworking men for no reason but the love of gold. Now, someone was trying to spoil a dream he hadn't even finished dreaming. Emmalene. Someone else wanted her. Wanted him to stay away from her. But he was staying away from her. He hadn't spoken to her of the things in his heart, though the intention was there, like a small kernel of a thought, working its way through the timid part of his brain toward the chamber of courage and into the compartment where determination and decisions were made.

He looked at the herd of cattle, scattered all over a greensward that undulated in the wind like a topaz sea, the evaporating dewdrops melting into invisibility, forming into little clouds that dotted the sky like stray sheep. God, he loved this country, and he wanted Emmalene to share it with him. He wanted her even more now, now that a man had died as a warning to him to stay away from her. His jaw hardened at the thought that another man with evil in his heart would want Emmalene, might woo her and take her away from him when he hadn't even mentioned that she had touched his heart and made him think of something he had never thought of before—marriage.

The word sounded alien to him, as if spoken by someone from a foreign land. He believed he had not heard the word since his own mother had spoken it, long ago, when she was alive and married to his father. She had treasured her marriage and spoke of her luck and joy in finding a man like his father and giving birth to his little sister and him.

He knew he was going to choke up if he kept thinking about what he had lost and what he may be about to lose.

He was worried about Carlos Montoya now, hoping that he had stayed in town, gotten a room in a fleabag hotel or rooming house and . . .

He shut off the thought about Carlos. What good was it to speculate where he might be or what he might be doing? One of his men was already dead, and no amount of speculation on his part could have foretold or prevented it.

Like Hobart and his gang, who had appeared out of nowhere, guns blazing, and shot dead everyone in their path. He and Ben were only alive because they had been up in the mine. They were unarmed and would have been shot dead just like all the others had they been seen.

As John and Ben approached with Cholo and the fallen Juanito, men started emerging from the bunkhouse and horses whinnied in the log barn they had built the summer before.

Gasparo Calderon shaded his eyes with his hand and stared at them without the slightest comprehension.

Benito joined Gasparo, fastening one suspender to his trousers, looking sleepy-eyed and turning his head to avoid damaging his eyes from the direct sunlight.

Smoke, a blue column of it, snaked from the cook shack's chimney and John knew that Ornery Dobbins was preparing breakfast for all of them. He felt a twinge of remorse for Benito. He was Juanito's first cousin and shared the same last name. Benito and Juan were more like brothers than cousins. They were very close and had grown up together in Sonora before coming to Colorado with a Basque sheepherder who had been killed by Utes near Durango.

Ben waved to Gasparo and Benito. Gasparo waved back. Benito started walking toward the cook shack, oblivious to the cargo draped across Cholo's saddle.

"What you got?" Gasparo said when he got within earshot of John and Ben.

Benito opened the door of the cook shack and disappeared.

"We got Juan," Ben said.

"Juanito? Did he fall asleep?"

"He's dead, Gasparo," Ben said. "His throat's cut."

"You don't mince words, do you, Ben?" John said dryly.

"Hell, it ain't no secret. I'm just glad Pepe ain't here."

Gasparo swore in Spanish, then crossed himself as if to absolve himself of his blasphemous outburst.

"Juanito, he's dead?"

"We got to lay him out and stitch up his neck," Ben said. "Before Benito sees him like this."

"What happened? John, you tell me, eh? You tell me what happened."

Gasparo was close to tears. He looked at Juanito's body but could not see his throat. The dead man was facedown in the saddle.

"Someone grabbed a calf and tortured it, I reckon," John said as he and Gasparo walked side by side. "When Juanito rode into the timber to check, the man jumped him and cut his throat."

"Why?" Gasparo almost choked on the word.

He was a burly man with a barrel chest, a face carved out of dark mahogany, and high cheekbones with a trace of vermilion highlighting the strong ridge bones underneath. His eyes were almost black, the color of ripe olives, and they were now misted with tears.

John turned back and shot Ben a look. He shook his head.

"We're still trying to figure that out," John said.

There was no need to mention the note or to bring Emma into it. Gasparo had enough to digest as it was. What was in the note was between him and Ben, and there was no need to make Juanito's murder any more complicated than it already was.

"Juanito, he never did nothing to nobody," Gasparo said as they neared the bunkhouse. There was anger in his voice now, anger at the injustice of Juan's death and hatred at the man who had taken his young compadre's life in such a brutal way.

Gasparo helped Ben untie the ropes and lift Juanito's body out of the saddle.

They laid the body behind the bunkhouse in the cool shade. Gasparo's eyes clouded up when he saw the gash in Juanito's throat. He knelt down beside the body, wept, and made the sign of the cross on his forehead and chest.

"Jesus," he murmured, in English.

"You got any needle and thread handy, Gasparo?" Ben asked.

"I will sew up the wound and wash him before Benito . . ."

But Benito was there. John tried to block his way, but he pushed past him and stared unbelievingly down at his cousin.

"Juan," he cried.

Gasparo stood up and faced the young man. He gripped Benito's arms with his hands and shook him.

"Do not look at him, Benito."

"What happened to Juanito?" Benito's querulous voice was almost a scream.

"He is dead," Gasparo said in Spanish.

"Who did this? Was it a bear? A cougar? My God, Juanito, do not die. Please do not die."

Then Benito fell to his knees and dropped his head onto Juanito's chest. He sobbed and squeezed his cousin with awkward arms. Gasparo put a hand on Benito's shoulder, knowing that he was powerless to console the grieving man.

John and Ben exchanged sad looks.

"Gasparo," John said. "There's something else you should know."

"Eh?" Gasparo turned his head to look at John.

"Montoya did not come back with the supply wagon last night. Ben and I are going to look for him."

Gasparo's face twisted into a grimace that was like a snarl.

"Que paso? Que en el Diablo paso? Que pasa aqui?"

"Maybe Montoya's all right," Ben said lamely.

Gasparo looked as if he wanted to kill someone just then. Anyone. His face was twisted in a horrible grimace and a snarl had settled on his mouth like an ugly stain. He doubled up his fists in frustration and his eyes looked as if they would pop out of their sockets like swollen liquid marbles.

"Calmate," John said, his voice a gentle whisper. "Stay steady, Gasparo. Benito needs you, and Juanito needs to go in the ground before the heat gets to him."

John's words seemed to calm Gasparo down.

He huffed a breath through his nostrils and unclenched his fists.

"Ben, you want to ride Cholo?" John said. "I'll saddle up Gent."

"Yeah, that'll save us time. You want grub to take with us? I can have Ornery slap together a couple of sandwiches."

John started to walk away around the side of the bunk-house.

"No," he said, his voice pitched low, "I hunt better on an empty belly."

He walked to the barn where his horse was in a stall, glad to slide out from under the thick grief that hovered over Juanito's body. When Benito had dropped to his knees, John had felt the full weight of that grief, that gray mantle that settled over him like a leaden blanket, blotting out all reason in its coarse fibers, smothering all rational thought.

He breathed deep of the air and yet knew that he, too, would grieve over Juanito, but in his own time and in his own way.

For now, he must think of the living and hope that Montoya was not in that dark place where Juanito had gone, that mysterious abyss where all men went and none returned.

4

BEN HITCHED CHOLO TO THE RAIL OUTSIDE THE BARN AND WALKED to the cook shack. When he opened the door, the smells of frying bacon, coffee, and beans assailed his nostrils. The walls of his stomach rippled, and he could practically hear the rumble of digestive juices.

There was a long table in the center of the room, the top of knotty pine so that Ben always had the feeling there were large eyes staring at him when he sat down to eat. Two benches were pulled out. These were made of tree stumps with whipsawed lumber nailed to their squared-off, resined tops. Salt and pepper shakers stood in the center of the table. Some of the pine knots had fallen out and the holes were filled with amber resin. Beyond the dining area was the kitchen, festooned with pots and pans hanging on dowels or hooks, a counter, sink, cupboards, and cabinets, Ornery's pride and joy.

Honore Dobbins looked at him from his position at the cookstove. They called him "Ornery" wherever he went be-

cause it was close enough to his name in the patois of the
West and it suited his personality at times. When he hauled
his chuck wagon on trail drives, he was not in the mildest
of moods when hungry drovers and wranglers clamored for
food.

"Ain't ready yet," Ornery said. "Where's John?"

"I didn't come in here for breakfast, Ornery. Can you
sack me up a couple of sandwiches, maybe some hardtack
and jerky?"

"You ask a lot of a man who's knee deep in the culinary
arts, Ben."

Ornery wore a big apron made of heavy denim, duck
trousers, and a pair of worn brogans on his feet. His graying
hair and beard were a snarl of unruly curls with tinges of
orange and black. His pudgy face was lumpy, as if dabs of
putty had been plastered to his cheeks and chin. His blue,
inset eyes missed very little behind the mounds of his cheekbones.

"I mean I need that grub real fast. Montoya didn't come
back last night and some bastard slit Juanito's throat. His
body's out behind the bunkhouse."

Ornery's mouth opened in surprise. He stroked his beard
as if that gave him security and stepped back from the
stove, a spatula in his hand.

"Boy, you sure know how to say good morning to a man,
don't you, Ben? That's more'n I can digest all at once."

"I'd be obliged," Ben said.

"Sure. I got a empty flour sack here somewhere's I can
fill. What the hell's goin' on, anyways?"

He opened a cabinet and took out a small sack that had
once contained pinto beans. He shook the dust off of it and
started opening cans where he stored jerky and hardtack.

"You'll get a butchered calf sometime this mornin', too."

Ornery carved slices out of bread he had baked the day before, slathered them with mustard and lifted beefsteaks from a pan on the stove and plopped them onto the bread.

"And I thought this would be an easy job," Ornery said as he packed the empty bean sack. "What with the women gone and all."

"Quit your bellyachin', Dobbins, you old coot. I'm the one dealin' with dead and missin' cowhands. All you have to do is eat that swill you fix for the hands."

Ornery grumped and handed the sack of food to Ben.

"I hope you find Montoya," he said, suddenly sobering.

"Yeah, me, too."

The sizzling bacon grabbed Ornery's attention, and he turned back to the stove. Smoke billowed up from the fry pan as he turned the bacon with his spatula. His face and beard were swallowed up in a cloud of steam as Ben walked out the door.

He put the grub in one of the saddlebags, slipped Juanito's rifle from the boot, and checked to see that it had a full magazine. He was just sliding the barrel back in its sheath when John emerged from the barn, leading Gent.

"You ready, Ben?" John asked.

"Ready as I'll ever be."

Gasparo rounded the corner of the bunkhouse and ran up to the two men as they were climbing into their saddles.

"John," he said, "Juanito, they torture him."

"What?" John said.

"His fingers. They are broke. I see them. Broke like sticks."

A shadow passed across John's face. His jaw hardened and his eyes narrowed to dangerous slits, like gunports cut into a tawny adobe wall. Ben's eyes widened and a tic in his cheek wobbled as if he had been struck with a sharp instrument.

"The screams," Ben murmured, loud enough for both of them to hear.

"Who does such a thing to Juanito, eh?" Gasparo said, tears wetting his eyes. "Juanito, he suffer much, I think."

"Gasparo," John said, "we'll get the man who did this to Juanito. You go back and take care of Benito. You and he have a grave to dig and a calf to skin out. You can't change what happened to Juanito."

"You will get the man who did this, John? You will torture him. You will break the fingers. You will make the man scream before you cut his throat."

An old biblical saying occurred to John as he listened to Gasparo's desperate plea. *Vengeance is mine, sayeth the Lord.* Juanito deserved vengeance. He could still hear those terrible screams, and now he knew where they had come from and why. Juanito's death was not the Lord's responsibility. The responsibility was his. He did not express those thoughts, but he knew the depth of Gasparo's feelings about Juanito's torture and death. He knew those feelings because they were his own, as well.

"We'll get him, Gasparo. Don't let your hate cloud your mind. Right now, Benito needs you. He needs you to be strong. And I need you. To take care of the dead and say your prayers over Juanito when you put him in the ground."

"You will get this man, John. You will bring him to me."

"Gasparo, you're not the only one here who wants justice for Juanito. Keep that in mind."

"I want to kill that man with my hands," Gasparo said, a bitterness in his voice that was like the sour taste of vinegar on a man's tongue.

"You sit tight, Gasparo. Be strong, for Benito. It is with the living that you must be concerned. Juanito is beyond pain now. Benito is the one who is hurting."

"And I," Gasparo said. "I hurt. I hurt much."

John did not say anything and Gasparo stood there, studying John's face. Satisfied, he turned and walked back toward the bunkhouse.

"He's takin' it hard, John," Ben said when Gasparo was out of earshot.

"We're all taking it hard, Ben."

"We ought to catch that bastard and bring him back here so Gasparo and Benito can cut the bastard to pieces real slow."

John ticked Gent's flanks with his spurs and turned him toward the pasture. He felt a change in the temperature as the sun rose higher and drew out the scents of the grass and the flowers, the curly hides of the cattle.

Ben and Cholo caught up with him as he rode toward the trail that led out of the valley, the trail where Montoya would have driven the supply wagon back the night before.

Many of the cattle in the herd were lined up at the creek while the grasses dried in the sun. Horned heads bobbed up and then bobbed back down, as each head drank. They would eat when the clover and alfalfa had lost their beads of dew and their fodder was warm and safe to eat. The gama grass and the grama were already dry, as was some of the bluestem. John and Ben had planted some of the seeds to blend with the native grasses, trying to achieve a lushness of fodder for the hungry herd. Some of the cattle bellowed as the riders passed, but the sounds were those of contentment, and John took them as such.

A flight of mourning doves flew past them, their gray bodies twisting, their wings whistling, as they headed from the timber to an unknown destination. A rabbit, nibbling on clover leaves, froze, then hopped away when the horses came too close. Somewhere, a chipmunk squeaked a warning and the creek made a sound like the splashing of a waterfall in the spring runoff, a soothing sound to John's ears as he thought about Juanito and vengeance.

Ben broke into his thoughts.

"I got me a bad feeling about Montoya," he said. "Why he didn't show up last night."

"Don't jump to conclusions, Ben."

"Hard not to, after what happened to Juanito."

"Thoughts like those can eat you alive, you let 'em," John said.

"Hell, what else is there to think about, Johnny?"

"Find something."

"We ain't out for no Sunday ride to meetin'."

"Might have taken Montoya a long time to unload Emma's furniture. You know how women are. She might have changed her mind about where to put her things a half dozen times."

"You got Emma on your mind, John?"

"I have a lot of things on my mind."

"Well, she's one of 'em."

"Maybe."

She was on his mind, along with Montoya. And he was trying not to think of Juanito and those last few moments of his life. Those moments of excruciating pain and, perhaps, knowing that he was going to die and could not do anything about it.

"Well, she's some woman, all right. I wonder about that note, tellin' you to stay away from her. Seems like she must have run into some bad company in town."

"Towns are full of bad company, Ben."

"Such a nice lady."

They reached the road and left the creek, angling down the twisting trail with its wagon ruts and dirt churned up by horses' iron hooves, descending through a corridor of pine trees and stands of aspen with their white trunks all aglow in the glare of the sun, their green leaves jiggling, changing shades of color as they twisted in the soft breeze streaming down from the mountains.

John hoped they would find Montoya in town or heading their way with the wagon full of the supplies he had ordered.

He hoped that Montoya was on his way back to the ranch, and he kept that hope until they rounded a bend in the road and saw the wagon, canted slightly with one wheel in a ditch, the horses standing forlorn and hipshot.

There was a dead silence and no sign of life as the two men approached what seemed like an abandoned wagon.

John felt something squeeze his heart, an intangible and disembodied pressure that stopped his breath for just a second or two.

One of the horses nickered. The other pawed the ground with its right hoof. The traces dangled lifelessly, black strands of leather that led to an empty seat.

Flies zizzed around in aimless circles above the wagon bed, their bodies glinting sparkles of blue and green. Gray deerflies arose from the horses' backs and left streaks of blood on their hides. The horses switched their tails and made little whispers that were as ominous as any John had ever heard.

Like whispers in an outdoor mausoleum.

5

CLOUDS FLOATED IN THE SKY. SMALL WISPS OF VAPOROUS ectoplasm attached themselves to the larger cumulus, the whiteness like fresh snowfall against the blue canopy. John breathed a deep breath as he nudged Gent toward the wagon. He scanned the ground, saw the hoof marks of a horse not attached to the wagon. He looked around and saw the boulders stacked high on both sides of the trail, the bushes in full leafing, sprouting in large clumps that added to walls of concealment where a man on horseback might hide until a lumbering wagon pulled the grade around the horseshoe curvature of the road.

His gut crawled with wormy undulations, rumbling on the emptiness therein, tightening and loosening folds of flesh, as if clawing for what might be called fear or just a morbid anticipation of something both horrible and unknown.

Ben made a sound in his throat as if he was trying to clear something distasteful out of his system or out of his mind. Then it was quiet, but John could hear the wood in the wagon creak or tick as the temperature changed again, from cool to warm, and the sound was annoying because it reminded John of deserted places, ghost towns, and old buffalo trails where the impressions of their hooves still scarred the earth. A feeling of emptiness assailed his senses as the ticking stopped, and he could hear the warm wind in his ears like a ghostly presence he could not see but only feel as if an invisible hand had touched him on the shoulder.

"John, it don't look good," Ben said, a sandy croak in his voice that was like the rasp of a feeding turkey.

"No, it doesn't," John murmured as if talking to himself.

"You gonna take a look in that wagon?" There was a trace of fear in Ben's voice. Fear of the unknown. Fear of discovering something diseased or unclean. A superstitious fear such as he might have had as a boy and that had now returned in the man.

"You wait," John said.

He rode alongside the wagon, his teeth clamped tight, his jaw rigid, as if he was about to face a nightmare in the golden haze of daylight. The muscles in his stomach tautened as his mind braced him for shock. He looked into the wagon bed, and there, amid the sacks of flour, sugar, and beans, the cans of coffee, and the sacks of oats and corn, Montoya lay sprawled like a broken scarecrow, his eyes glassed over with the frost of death, staring up at a blue sky clotted with clouds, and a hideous grin across his throat, gaping like a clown's mask, flies nipping at the dried blood, the sizzling sounds of their wings assaulting John's ears with the indecency of their hunger.

"I found Montoya," he said as he turned to look at Ben. Ben sat his horse like a man turned to stone, stiff and stolid as a statue.

"He's dead, ain't he?" Ben stammered.

John heard the sizz-sawing of the flies in B-flat minor,

watched them crawl across the wound and crawl in and out
of Montoya's nostrils.

"Yes. His body's stiff already. So he must have been killed
yesterday afternoon or early evening, the way I figure it."

"How?"

"Throat cut. Same as Juanito."

"Christ," Ben said. He rode up to the wagon beside John
and looked into the bed.

He took off his hat and batted at the cloud of flies above
the wagon bed. They scattered like a spilled tray of a print-
er's punctuation marks, then clustered again, tracking the
odors of death, diving down into putrefying flesh with tiny
antennae and big, multifaceted eyes protruding from their
tiny black heads.

He saw the slash in Montoya's throat and something else.

"His mouth," Ben said. "It looks kinda funny."

John reached down and touched Montoya's mouth. It
looked swollen, and when he pried the lips apart, he saw
something inside. He tugged and pulled out a handkerchief.
The cloth was folded up into a ball. The outer layer was stiff
with dried saliva, and the wad that had been deep in his
throat was spattered with rusty dots of blood, as if he had
choked when his throat was opened like a sliced watermelon. He stuffed it in his pocket, then lifted one of Montoya's hands. He heard something click when he moved two
or three of the dead man's fingers.

"Broken," he said.

"Just like Juanito's," Ben said.

John looked at Montoya's other hand. It was twisted as
if he had died in great pain. All of his fingers and his thumb
appeared to be broken as well.

"Montoya died a hard death," John said. "The man who
did this must have asked him where our ranch was. I figure

Montoya held out as long as he could. Looks like all of his fingers are broken."

"Maybe that bastard just likes to torture people before he kills 'em," Ben said.

John set Montoya's mangled hand down gently on his stomach.

It was difficult to imagine what kind of man would do such a thing to Montoya and then again to Juanito. *Maybe,* he thought, *a man without a conscience.* Or a man who enjoyed watching people suffer. He must have held a gun to Montoya's head, then gagged him until he was ready to talk. He must have broken each finger, one by one, while Montoya screamed in pain and writhed in agony.

"Vengeance," John murmured.

"Huh? What'd you say, John?"

"Nothing. I just want to kill whoever did this to Montoya."

"And Juanito."

"Yeah. And Juanito."

"Killin's not good enough," Ben said. "I want whoever did this to suffer like them poor boys did."

"That's a thought," John said. "An eye for an eye."

Ben looked at Montoya again.

"They's somethin' stickin' out of his shirt pocket. See it? Looks like paper."

John saw it.

"Another note, maybe." He leaned out of the saddle and reached across Montoya's body. He pulled a small scrap of paper from the slain man's pocket. It was torn from a small notebook and looked to be just like the one he had found on Juanito's body.

"Same handwriting," John said as he looked at the note.

"What's it say?"

John read the note aloud:

"I know where you live, Savage. You keep away from Emmalene. She's a Blanchett for as long as she lives. You stay away from her or you won't live long."

"He makes it pretty plain," Ben said.

"He gave himself away with this one, Ben."

"Oh? How so?"

"He says *she's a Blanchett.*"

"Well, that's her name, ain't it?"

"Her married name, yes. But she's a widow and I killed her husband."

"You goin' somewhere with this, Johnny?"

"Who would lay claim to a widow woman except someone kin to Argus Blanchett?"

"I don't know. A brother, maybe. You'd have to ask Emma, I reckon."

"That's just what I'm going to do, Ben. Anyway, this note might give us some kind of clue that will lead us to the man who killed Juanito and Montoya. If he's kin to Argus, there's a chance I can find him."

"Ain't no law in Butterfly Creek."

"No, and there wasn't any law when Ollie Hobart and his gang slaughtered all of our people."

"And we planted 'em all six feet under," Ben said.

John tucked the note in his pocket with the other one. Maybe Emma would recognize the handwriting or have an idea of what the man meant about her being a Blanchett.

"What are you goin' to do next, John?"

"You'll have to take Montoya and the wagon back up to the ranch. See that he gets a proper burial. I'm going into town to see Emma."

"By yourself? That don't sound good to me, John."

"You can meet me there later if you're worried."

"Damned right I'm worried. Where do I meet you?"

"Emma's house. Or, if she's working, I'll be at Cooper's General Store."

"I don't like it none, John. You goin' into that poor excuse for a town all by yourself."

"I've got this," John said, patting the butt of his pistol.

"Yeah, and you might get shot in the back by a murderin' bastard you don't even know."

"I could fall off Gent and break my neck, too."

"You could do that. Ain't likely, though."

"And, it's not likely the man I'm looking for knows what I look like. If I've never seen him, he probably has never seen me."

"Hell, he could be anybody."

"He probably didn't know where we live if he had to torture Montoya to find out."

"You got a point. A small point, John."

"Get cracking, Ben. Tie Cholo to the wagon and drive it back to the ranch. I'll see you in town, maybe."

"I don't like it none," Ben grumbled.

"You said that. Now get to it."

Savage slid out of the saddle and handed his reins to Ben.

"What're you going to do, John? Take a leak?"

"Look around. Maybe the man's tracks can tell me something. See, that's where he stepped off his horse. Left boot prints in a couple of spots."

Ben looked around uneasily.

"It's right spooky here," he said as he watched John step carefully among the various horse and boot prints around the back of the wagon. He put his hat back on and took off his bandanna and wiped the dirt rings on his neck, sopping up gobs of sweat in the process. He retied the bandanna around his neck and looked everywhere but in the wagon bed.

John hunkered down, squatting on his haunches to examine the clear prints of boots. They were not distinctive but seemed to indicate a man of medium stature, weighing about a hundred and fifty or a hundred and sixty pounds. He gauged that figure from the depth of the imprint.

He walked around the wagon, then followed his and Ben's tracks for thirty yards or so, came back, and walked off the same distance behind the wagon.

"Two men rode up here," he told Ben. "One rode on up toward the ranch. The other turned around and went back to town or wherever these bastards came from."

"You can tell all that from lookin' at them tracks."

"I wonder why he sent the other man back," John said.

"Didn't need him no more, maybe."

"Maybe. It looks like they might have followed Montoya from town and just picked this spot because Montoya had to slow the team down around this curve in the road."

"So, two men follered Montoya, and then one of 'em went back to town?"

"Whoever killed Montoya probably asked him questions about how many hands were on night herd and how many men were at the ranch."

"You're makin' this jasper out to be a pretty smart sonofabitch."

"I'd say he can add a figure or two."

Ben snorted, swiped a hand at a phalanx of gray deerflies.

John stood still for several moments. Ben could see that he was thinking. The horses switched their tails and the flies continued to swarm and feed on dried blood and Ben's sweat.

"The man who killed Juanito rode a horse with one shoe worn and one of the heels broken off. The other man rode a bigger horse and was heavier. He never stepped down, but probably held a gun on Montoya while the other man tortured and killed him."

"Hmm," said Ben.

John climbed back into the saddle.

"See you, Ben. You've got a heap to do when you get back to the ranch. Have Benito and Gasparo help you unload the wagon and see that they bury Montoya and keep their eyes open."

"You think that killer's goin' to come back real soon?"

"No. He gave me his warning. Now he'll wait like a spider at the center of its web for me to come after him."

"He's that smart, eh?"

"He's probably looking after Emma to see if I heeded his warning."

John settled in the saddle and looked off at the distant peaks that were mantled in snow.

"John, if you kill him before I get to town, you kill him real slow, will you?"

"Let's not jump the gun on this, Ben."

"Seems to me that's just what you're doin'."

John turned Gent and rode off down the trail. He studied the tracks of the horse the man rode. One hind shoe was worn at the edge, and one heel flange seemed to be missing. That was enough for him to identify the horse. But it was his guess that the animal would need shoeing before long. After that, it would be almost impossible to identify the horse.

Butterfly Creek was not that big of a town. If the man he was hunting was a saloon drinker or stayed in a hotel or put his horse up in a stable, he would find him.

And if there was a blacksmith in town, he could check with him and find out who owned the horse with a worn shoe and a busted stud at the heel.

In the back of his mind, though, nestling there like a burr

under a saddle blanket, was the nagging idea that Emma knew who the man was. Who was he? And what was his connection with Emma?

Those questions nagged at him all the way into the dirty little town on the flat where the creek ran through a plain flattened by ancient floods long before the white man came west to plunder and spoil a perfect place of silence and grandeur.

6

EMMA AND EVA SPENT THEIR EVENING ARRANGING THE FEW items of furniture Montoya had brought down from the ranch and unloaded. There was a small table, some packed vases, two chairs, a lantern, some pillows and bedsheets, a stuffed leather hassock, a worn footstool, a dresser, and a small bureau. The clapboard house was bigger than the cabin Argus had built her, but she didn't like the smell of it, the smell of Butterfly Creek that wafted through the rows of houses behind the main street.

The house she rented from Jesse Cooper, her boss at the mercantile store that bore his name, had been built well beyond the last row of houses in a clearing surrounded by aspen, small pines, and some fir trees. Cooper had built it for himself and his wife, but she had died, and he had moved into a hotel rather than hire a housekeeper.

Emma lit the lamp in her living room when the sun went down after Montoya left.

"I'll plant flowers, Eva. It won't be so bad here."

"I hate it," Eva said, exhausted from cutting firewood for their small fireplace and chopping sage and kindling all afternoon. Her mother put the fronds of sage on the fire at night so that she would not have to smell the town. She also dabbed herself with perfume every night, behind her ears, under her armpits, and between her legs.

"The flowers will make it nice," her mother said.

The sun was starting to set and the pines and piñons she could see through the front window glowed with a peach fire, the shadows long across the yard in the shapes of spires and parapets, obelisks and church towers. Eva watched her mother standing there in contemplation and felt the sadness in her, the loneliness that she also felt. She had loved living in the mountains, close to the sky, with the fragrance of pine and spruce and fir in her nostrils, the comforting musk of the cattle feeding on the lush grass, and the howl of a timber wolf at night far up some lonesome canyon. She missed the liquid voices of the Mexicans and the gravelly voice of Ben Russell and the soft, deep voice of John Savage, the cooing of mourning doves in the trees every morning and the lowing of cattle at night.

"Ma," Eva said, "you miss him, don't you?"

Her mother turned away from the window, her blue eyes bright in the lamplight, the trees fading behind her through the window.

"Who?"

"You know who."

Her mother walked over to the small divan where Eva sat, her legs tucked beneath her like storks' legs, her green calico dress draping over her knees that were skinned from kneeling in gravel to fill the water buckets.

"He killed your father, Eva. My husband."

"Yes, in self-defense. Daddy was a mean man. He treated you like dirt."

"You must not speak ill of the dead."

"Well, I wish John Savage was my real father."

Emma lifted her hand to slap her daughter but thought better of it.

"Were you going to hit me, Mama?"

"You shouldn't talk like that, Eva."

"You like him, don't you? I mean you like John a lot."

"Never mind. He's not interested in me." There was a wistfulness to Emma's tone, and her eyes appeared to lose their sparkle for a moment. She lowered her hand and sat down beside her daughter. She breathed a sigh and shook her head as if answering an unspoken question of her own.

"I should start the fire," she said, idly, a dreamy expression on her pale face.

"He likes you, Mama," Eva blurted out after a few moments of silence.

Emma's head snapped around, and she stared at Eva as if her daughter had uttered a sacrilegious oath.

"You don't know that," Emma retorted. Then her lips tightened down so that they formed a thin, bloodless seam.

"I've seen the way he looks at you, Ma. And the way you look at him."

"I don't look at him in any way."

"Yes, you do. And so does he. When you're not watching him, he looks at you."

"He's just not used to women is all," Emma said defensively. "He's a bachelor."

"And you're a widow woman. You're still young enough to marry again."

"Marry? Never!"

"Oh, Mama. I never saw you look at Daddy that way."

"What way?" Emma patted her hair, suddenly self-conscious, as if Eva had discovered a dark secret, as if her daughter had been able to look into her heart and mind. It was a disconcerting thought.

"Whenever you see John, your eyes get real bright and sometimes I see you blush when he compliments you on how you look. At times, you look like a girl. Like a girl my own age. You get flustered when he's around, and when he leaves you look real sad sometimes. You looked real sad when we rode away from the ranch and both of you waved good-bye to each other."

"Oh, nonsense, Eva."

"No. I know what I see."

"Ah, the fantasies of the young. Especially young girls. You're not quite eighteen and you think you know everything about the world."

"I know enough."

Emma laughed, but her laughter was forced, and she knew that Eva had been watching her and watching John Savage. And Eva had, perhaps, seen the longing she had for John to take her in his arms and kiss her and hold her tight until their heartbeats mingled in a common rhythm. It was a secret. It was her secret, and she meant to keep it until all desire faded away, as she knew it must. She had her own life to live and a daughter to raise. John had his ranch, and Ben, and besides, he was the kind of man who had no time for a woman. He was just too independent. Too set in his ways.

"I'm going to light the fire," Emma said, rising from the divan. "It's getting right chilly in here."

"Sure, Ma. Run away. That's what you always do when John gets close to you and looks at you with those deep brown eyes of his."

Emma walked to the fireplace, took a box of lucifers off

the mantel, and knelt down. There was squaw wood beneath sticks of thin kindling wood. She struck a match and touched the flame to the crushed dry bundle of squaw wood gathered from the lower branches of the pine trees. The wood caught and flared, the orange-and-yellow tongues licking the kindling, blackening the blanched wood. As the kindling blazed, she added two logs on top, and these, too, began to blacken and burn.

She stood up and backed away from the heat. She put the matchbox back on the mantel. Smoke rose up in the chimney and the room began to warm. She looked out the front window next to the door and saw the gray loaves of clouds above the town, their lower edges streaked with the color of salmon, sprays of light lingering in the sky like the fragile and fading glow of sunbeams shining through a stained-glass church window. As she watched, the clouds turned to ashes floating into the somber blackness of oncoming night.

"I'll fix supper," Emma said.

Eva pouted on the couch, looking out at the darkening sky, her face lit by firelight, her pigtails shining like the wing feathers of blackbirds.

Emma glanced at her and heaved a short sigh. She went into the kitchen and lifted the glass chimney of a lamp, turned up the oil valve. She struck a match and dabbed flame on the wick.

Just then, there was a knock on the door. Emma, startled, blew out the match.

"I'll get it," Eva said.

"No, you sit right there. I'll see who it is."

Emma walked with brisk steps to the door and opened it. Her hand moved close to the ax handle she kept next to it.

"Good evening, Miss Emmalene," a young boy said. He stood there with his cap in his hand. Emma recognized him. He worked as a stock boy at the store.

"What is it, Kevin?"

"Mr. Cooper wants you at the store right away."

"But I was off hours ago."

"He decided to do inventory and he says he needs you real bad." Kevin backed up, away from the door. "And real quick," he said.

Then the boy was gone, running through the dusk as if school had just let out and he was in a hurry to get home.

"Oh, dear," Emma said as she closed the door. "What am I going to do about supper?"

"I can fix my own, Ma," Eva said, rising from the couch. "This means extra money, don't it?"

"Doesn't it," Emma corrected her. "Yes, I suppose so. Jesse picked a fine time to do inventory. I'll be there all night. Do you want to come and help me?"

"No, Ma. I don't feel too good and I'm real tired."

"You lock these doors and keep them locked, do you hear? I'll get back home as soon as I can."

"I'll get your coat and a shawl, Ma."

Eva ran into the bedroom and returned with her mother's shawl, her coat, and her purse.

"I'll eat something at the store," Emma said as she slipped into her coat. She wrapped the shawl around her neck and shoulders. "Don't forget to bank the fire when you go to bed."

"I won't," Eva said, pushing her mother out the door. "Don't you worry none, Ma."

"Good-bye."

"Bye-bye, Mama," Eva said and went to the door after her mother disappeared down the street. She closed and locked it.

She walked into the kitchen. She was feeling poorly and wasn't hungry. She turned down the wick until there was just a faint light in the room. She looked out the back window. The trees were just black shadows, ominous shapes that could have been anything, human or animal. She shivered with a tinge of fright and walked quickly back into the front room.

Emma worked all night and into the morning. She was perspiring and exhausted when Jesse Cooper told her to go home.

"I'll keep the store closed this afternoon," he told her. "Come back around five and we'll finish up. There'll be some sugar in your pay this week."

"Thank you, Jess," she said and hurried out the door and down the street.

Before she even entered her house, Emma knew something was wrong. She could feel it. She didn't know what it was, but she ran the last few feet to her door and fumbled in her purse for her key. She put it in the lock, but the door opened when she put her hand on the doorknob. The leather hinges creaked as the door swung open.

"Eva," she called as she rushed through the door and into the front room. "Eva, I'm home."

There was no answer.

The fire in the fireplace had gone out. The lamp was still burning with a feeble flame. The room was cold and the house creaked with emptiness.

Frantically, Emma ran into Eva's small bedroom. Empty. She ran to the back door. Locked, the latch still down. The house was cold. And bleak.

She looked in her own bedroom. The covers were taut and untouched.

There was a piece of paper in the center of her bed.

She rushed to it and picked it up. She began to read and then crumpled to the floor in a heap, sobbing with no control over the flood of tears.

She was still crying when she heard hoofbeats outside.

Then she heard someone come through the door, calling out her name.

Emma shrieked as if she had just been snatched from the slavering jaws of death. The shriek died away as the doorway filled with the shape of a man, a six-gun on his hip, his pants and shirt, hat, and boots covered with a thin patina of trail dust.

Then she fainted.

7

JOHN SAVAGE STOOD IN THE DOORWAY FOR ONLY A SECOND OR two.

He looked down at Emma. She looked like a broken flower, with her dress spread like a fan around her, her shawl drooping over her coat. Her face was streaked with the tracks of her tears, her blue eyes bulging from red-rimmed sockets, her mouth wide open.

John rushed in and knelt down in front of her. He held a large key in his hand. He held it up close to her face.

"You drop this?" he said, his voice velvet-soft with concern.

Emma's first instinct was to laugh, but the chuckle died in her throat before it could reach her lips. Instead, she reached out for John with both arms, grabbed him, and pulled herself into his embrace. She heard the key fall to the floor with a dull clank. She shivered with relief as he squeezed her tight.

"Oh, John, Evangeline's gone," she sobbed, her head embedded in his chest.

He stroked her hair with one hand.

The soothing touch of his hand seemed to calm her. She drew back and looked up into his deep brown eyes. They had never been this close before, and she heard the pounding throb of her heart in her ear. An electric tingling coursed through her body, and she gasped for a full breath, breaking through a last forlorn sob.

"Emma," he said, "what happened here? Were you attacked by someone?"

She shook her head.

"Eva's gone," she said. "Kidnapped." She raised her head to look into his eyes. Her own were swimming in fresh tears. "I—I worked all night. Just got home and she was gone. There was . . . there was a note on my bed."

He helped her to her feet. There, on the floor next to the bed, was the note. John reached down and picked it up.

He recognized the handwriting. The note was written in the same hand as those he had found on Juanito and Carlos.

Emma leaned against him, rereading the note in John's hands. A chilling shudder coursed through her body.

Emma, you wasn't here, the note read, *so I took Eva. You meet me in Denver at the Larimer Hotel on Larimer street. If you don't come in two days, you won't never see Eva again.*

"Oh, John, he's going to kill her," Emma sobbed.

"Who wrote this, Emma?"

"My husband's brother. He got out of prison a month ago and came to see me."

"Argus's brother?"

"Yes. His name is Fergus. He's not a twin, but they look and act alike. Fergus is meaner than Argus ever was. He—he killed a man in Texas. They sent him to Huntsville prison for ten years. He and Argus were real close."

"What did he want?" John asked.

"He wanted me," she said.

"Why?"

"He said whatever Argus owned was now his. He heard about his brother's death in Denver and came here, looking for me."

"You should have told me. Did Eva know about him?"

Emma shook her head.

"He came to Cooper's, where I work, to find out where I was, and I was actually there. I—I didn't tell him where I lived."

John sensed that Emma was not telling him everything. She had not told her daughter. That was a mistake. And now, he felt that she was holding back. Holding back on something important.

"Did you tell him where you used to live?" he asked.

"I—I don't know what you mean."

"Yes, you do. Did you tell him about me and my ranch?"

She stepped away from him as if seized by a sudden impulse to retreat from his questioning.

"I—I might have said something. I was so flustered, so upset when he came into the store and asked me to go to Denver and live with him. I was shocked. And I was afraid."

"Did you tell him my name?" John said, and there was a hardness in his voice as if his words were cut from a block of heavy lead.

"John . . ."

"What did you tell him, Emma?"

"I—he—he caught me off guard. I—I didn't know what to say. I just wanted him to go away and leave me alone."

"Answer my question." He fixed her with a hard look through narrowed eyes, a look that made her wince inside as if she had been pierced by twin darts.

"I told him I was betrothed," she said.

"To me?"

"Yes."

"And, you told him my name and where I lived."

"No, I didn't tell him where you lived. I—I did say your name. John, I just had to get rid of him. I thought he would go away if I told him you and I were going to be married."

"What did he say to that?"

"Let's get out of this room. I can smell him in here."

They walked to the front room. Emma was wringing her hands, gazing out the window at his horse, staring at the open door. She closed it, sat on the divan. John stood over her, looking down as she continued to wring her hands.

"He got very angry," she said. "He told me I had no right to marry anybody but him. I told him he was the last man I would ever marry."

"And he left the store then?"

"No. He threatened me. He said if I married you that I'd be twice a widow. He said . . ." She bent over then and began weeping again. She held her face in her hands. Her body shook and he sat down beside her, put an arm around her shoulders.

"Take a deep breath," he said. "He's not here now. He can't hurt you. What else did he say?"

"He—he said he'd kill you if he ever saw you with me," she sobbed. "Oh, John, I'm sorry. I'm sorry I ever married Argus. I'm sorry I got you into this. I've got to go to Denver. I've got to find Eva."

"You couldn't help it, Emma. Does Fergus look like his brother?"

"Yes. He's a year or two older. But they could almost be taken for twins. Fergus, I think, was in love with me and took it hard when I married his brother."

"So, now he thinks he has a right to claim you."

"I—I guess so."

"Who did he kill down in Texas, Emma?"

She raised her head and looked at him with wild eyes. They rolled around in their sockets. She looked terrified, as if awaking from a horrible nightmare.

"Oh, John, don't ask me any more questions. Please. I've got to go. My horse is at the livery stables. I've got to get to Denver."

"I'll ride to Denver. I'll get Eva back."

"No, no," she said, her voice rising to a pitch that bordered on hysteria. "He'll kill her the minute he sees you."

"He doesn't know what I look like. He doesn't know me."

"The man has a sixth sense, John. He would know the minute he saw you. He would know who you were."

"You won't get Eva back by yourself, Emma. He'll take you and her wherever he wants to go."

"I—I . . ."

"You know what I say is true. If you go there, he'll have both of you. You can't fight him alone. You can't beat him."

"Maybe we could trick him. Sometime, somewhere. When he's least expecting it, Eva and I could run away from him and hide where he'd never find us."

"Do you really believe that?"

She didn't say anything for a long while. He could see the torment in her eyes, the inner anguish that was tearing her apart as if she were a rag doll in the mouth of a ferocious pit bull.

"No. He's very possessive. He'd kill us both if we tried to run away from him."

"You stay here. I'll go after Fergus and bring Eva back."

"I couldn't stand being here alone and not knowing. Please take me with you."

He drew in a breath, considered her plea. It was a long ride to Denver. They couldn't make it in one day. But once there, she might prove helpful in coaxing Fergus out in the open. If he thought she was alone, he might let down his guard. It was still a risky proposition. But it might work, if they were both careful.

"I have a score of my own to settle with Fergus Blanchett," he said.

"What? What are you talking about?"

"I think he killed two of my men. Men you knew."

"Who?"

"Juanito and Carlos."

"Fergus killed them? When?"

"Yesterday and last night. He left notes on their bodies warning me to stay away from you. Same handwriting as in that note he left for you."

She gasped. She buried her face in both hands.

"Oh, John. He—he's a horrible, horrible, man."

"He's a killer, and now he has your daughter."

"Will you take me with you?"

"We'll have to get bedrolls. I didn't bring mine."

"I have Eva's and mine here. All I have to do is pack some food and go to the livery and get my horse. You'll come with me."

"Yes," he said.

While she packed food for them and gathered up two bedrolls, John looked around the house and in Eva's room. He didn't know what he was looking for, but he wondered if Fergus had been alone when he came to Emma's and kidnapped Eva. He had a hunch that at least two men had barged in and overpowered the young lady.

One was Fergus, sure enough. The other was large, heavyset, and probably just as mean and cold-blooded as Fergus.

He didn't say anything to Emma about that second man whose tracks he had seen on the road.

She had enough to worry about.

And, as a matter of fact, so did he.

He got a piece of paper from Emma and a pencil. He wrote out a note for Ben and nailed it on the outside of the front door.

Ben, he wrote, *Emma and I are on our way to Denver. The Larimer Hotel. See you there. Hurry.*

He signed his name, although he knew it was unnecessary.

A half hour later he and Emma rode out of Butterfly Creek and down toward the main road to Denver. In the distance he could see Pikes Peak, its snowy crag rising to the white clouds above it, and to the east, the prairie stretching as far as the eye could see, all green and brown, with clumps of sage and prickly pear, yuccas in full bloom, the spikes of Spanish bayonets gleaming in the sun.

He looked at Emma, riding alongside him on her steeldust gray, and felt a melting inside him, as if something had squeezed his heart and it was leaking sweet maple syrup that he could taste on the tip of his tongue.

8

THE BIG MAN'S NAME WAS JUBAL ROGAN. HE STOOD BETTER THAN six feet, with a wrestler's beefy arms, a neck thick as a ten-pound ham, and powerful legs that were bowed like swollen calipers. He had thick short hair the color of straw atop a bee-stung face so lumpy it might have been plastered over his skull with putty. His porcine eyes were sunk in fat and were as pale as opals, flanking a hooked nose that had been broken so many times it looked like a mashed glob of desiccated clay.

Eva's arms were wrapped around his thick waist, her hands tied there to hold her fast as she rode behind Rogan. Fergus had done that after putting her on Rogan's horse, a sturdy dun with a cropped mane that went by the name of Sandy. Fergus had taken the gag out of her mouth as soon as they had left Butterfly Creek behind them. They rode a game trail down to the flat and stayed well away from, but in sight of, the road to Denver.

Fergus rode ahead of Rogan on a coal-black gelding he called Jet. It had belonged to his brother, Argus, and, with its three gaits, suited him. He was a lean, muscled man with a prison pallor, dark hair, and large brown eyes. He wore a gray shirt, striped black-and-gray pants, boots that had long since lost their shine and were the color of faded blood. He had a firm set to his jaw, but his mouth was small and wizened, his lips cracked, as if he had chewed mouthfuls of thumbtacks for several years.

After riding all night, Fergus called a halt. He untied Eva's hands and pulled her to the ground.

"I have to pee," she said.

"Go on then," Fergus said. "But if you run, I'll break both your legs."

"I won't run. Why are you doing this, Uncle Fergus?"

"None of your damned business."

Eva walked over to where several clumps of sagebrush grew and squatted down. Fergus rolled a cigarette and watched her out of the corner of his eye. Rogan took a leak right out in the open, and Eva turned her head so that she wouldn't have to see him.

She was still in shock from the night before when she had heard the knock on her door. She had thought it was her mother and opened it. Fergus and Jubal had rushed in before she could close the door and keep them out. Jubal had grabbed her with those big arms of his.

"Where's your ma?" Fergus had demanded.

"She—she's up in the mountains," Eva'd lied. "Where we used to live."

"That bitch," Fergus had said.

"Let me go," Eva'd told Jubal, but he'd held her fast. She had felt like an animal caught in a trap.

"You ain't goin' nowhere," Fergus had said. Then he had

roamed through the house, his boots clomping on the floor, slamming doors and raging about her mother, cursing and pounding the walls with his fists.

"She won't be back for a week," Eva said when Fergus came back into the room.

"Well, she'll have a surprise or two if she went up to the Savage ranch," Fergus had replied. "And she'll damn sure have a surprise here when she gets back."

Eva had watched him write a note on a piece of paper and carry it into her mother's bedroom. Then he and Jubal had taken her outside.

"Where are you taking me?" she'd asked.

"Goin' to Denver. You've growed a heap since I last seen you, Evangeline. You were just a tot on your daddy's knee."

"I hate you, Uncle Fergus. Let me go."

Fergus had slapped her then, slapped her so hard her ear rang, and then he lifted her up on a horse behind Jubal and pulled her arms around the big man's waist and tied her hands.

They spent the night well off the road. Fergus tied her feet, and both men took turns standing guard over her. She shivered from the cold all night even though Jubal had put a blanket over her.

The next morning they stopped near Castle Rock just as dawn was graying and the sky was turning murky in the half-light.

She rubbed her wrists as she walked back to where Fergus was standing, smoking a cigarette. Jubal buttoned his pants and grinned at her. He looked like a big ape, she thought, and she stuck her tongue out at him to show her contempt.

"You do that again," Fergus said, "and I'll slap you silly."

"Ma will kill you, Uncle Fergus. She can shoot a gun."

"Hell, I know that. Me'n Argus taught her."

"She'll shoot you dead."

"Nope, little gal, she won't shoot me. She'll marry me."

"Oh, you, you filthy man. You stink."

Fergus slapped Eva hard across the face. She staggered away from him and was about to fall when Jubal grabbed her. She fought to get away from him, and he let her go.

Eva did not want to cry, but her face hurt so much she could not control her tears. She clamped her lips together and glared with defiance at Fergus. Tears streamed from her eyes and cascaded down her cheeks. She touched a hand to the red spot that was blooming like a flower on her face.

"You're so cruel," she said to Fergus. "I hate you."

"Eva, you don't know what hate is. I do. I grew up on hate, and I eat hate for breakfast every day. I go to sleep with hate. I wake up with it. You hate being hurt, but that ain't real hate. Hate is something you build your life on and it puts iron in your muscles."

She kept silent, surprised at what her uncle had just said. She had disliked her father because of his cruelty to her mother, but her uncle was a far more despicable man. He exuded evil; she could almost feel it oozing from him like some invisible plague. She shrank away from him and turned her head so that she would not have to look at his face and see his wicked mouth, those burning eyes.

"Fergus, we got to get on," Jubal said.

Fergus puffed on his cigarette and watched the shadows crawl down the face of Castle Rock as the sun rose higher in the east. It was a raging ball of reddish orange fire, lighting the thin rows of clouds hovering over the horizon, turning their gray shapes into silvery blossoms floating in a milky sea.

"What about Bobbitt?" Jubal asked as Fergus dropped his cigarette to the ground and stepped on it with his boot heel.

"Watch what you say around her," Fergus said, nodding in Eva's direction.

"Well, we ain't makin' no money chasin' after these women."

"Dick and Fred are keeping an eye on Bobbitt for us. The longer we wait, the more we'll have waiting for us. Now, get up on your horse and keep your mouth shut."

Jubal climbed onto his horse. Fergus lifted Eva up behind him. Jubal reached back and grabbed her hands, pulled her arms around his back. Fergus tied her wrists together with the heavy twine.

He looked up at her and tilted his hat back.

"You do any screamin' when we get to Denver, the gag goes back in your mouth. You got that?"

"I won't scream," she said.

As she looked at him, he patted the hilt of the big bowie knife hitched to his belt.

"If you do scream, Eva," Fergus said, "it'll be your last. This knife's got razor-sharp edges on both sides."

She shuddered at the thought of having her throat cut with that big knife.

Fergus mounted his horse and they rode off toward Denver.

The sun cleared the eastern horizon and drenched the long prairie with dazzling light and searing heat. Eva's stomach groaned with hunger, and perspiration leaked from the pores in her armpits and along her hairline. It was uncomfortable riding on the horse's rump, but at least they were not at a gallop.

Off to her left, she saw a heavy wagon lumbering along the road toward Denver. She read the legend on the side: BOBBITT FREIGHT LINES. There was lettering underneath, but she couldn't make it out. The wagon was pulled by a team of four horses. It was traveling slightly faster than they were. She watched it until it was out of sight.

The name sounded familiar and then she remembered that Jubal had mentioned it back in the shadow of Castle Rock. Bobbitt. Was there a connection? She didn't know, but she knew she would remember it. She was sure it meant something. Something her uncle and Jubal had more than a passing interest in.

Sweat dripped into her eyes and stung them with acid. She closed them and rubbed her forehead on Jubal's back. The smell of him made her sick to her stomach, but there was nothing in it to come up. She was hungry and tired. They had not slept all night under the stars, only a couple of hours, and she felt the weight of sleeplessness descend on her, draining her of energy, sapping her muscles of strength. Her arms ached and her wrists itched where the twine bound them. Her fingers turned numb, and she thought her blood must be pooling up in her fingers, making them thick and lifeless as dried gherkins.

She was nearly mad with hunger when they left the outskirts of Denver and rode down a maze of narrow, nearly empty streets, until they came to a large boulevard at dusk. They turned onto a street that was glittering with streetlamps and windows glowing with yellow light.

Jubal pulled up to a building with a large front. The sign said LARIMER HOTEL. It was at the end of a dark block and looked old in the twilight. Fergus dismounted and wrapped his reins around the hitchrail. Then he untied her and pulled her from Jubal's horse. Her legs were so weak she could scarcely stand, and Fergus had to hold her up.

"We'll get some grub in you," he said, his voice low and gravelly. "Stretch your legs to get the blood going again."

Jubal dismounted and tied up his horse.

"Go in and get the key," Fergus said. "We'll go on up in a minute or two."

"Will do," Jubal said. He entered the hotel. Eva saw his back through the window as he went to the desk.

Fergus walked her around in a small circle.

"Remember," he said. "You keep your mouth shut or this bowie knife goes right into your back."

"Ummm," she mumbled. Her legs began to respond. She felt the blood flow into them. Her empty stomach made her feel hollow. She was light-headed and thought she might faint, but Fergus grabbed her hand and started toward the double doors of the seedy hotel. She heard music, guitars and fiddles, floating from somewhere down the street. The streetlamps and the lights in the windows blurred as she went inside. The clerk was not there and the lobby was empty.

Fergus pulled her along with him as he made long strides to reach the stairs. She stumbled up them as he held on to her with an arm around her waist. She saw a dark hallway and, from an open door, a light suddenly appeared as Jubal lit a lamp.

She and Fergus entered the musty-smelling room. Her feet felt dead and her legs wobbled beneath her.

"This is your home until your ma comes for you," Fergus said. He closed the door behind them. Jubal walked up and she heard a key turn in the lock.

She staggered to a small couch and sat down. She rubbed her forehead and felt the grit of salt from the dried sweat.

"Jubal, get us some grub and a bottle of whiskey," Fergus said.

"You want Messican or Chinese?"

"Mexican," Fergus said. "Something that will stick to our ribs."

"I'll get us some pie, too."

"I expect little Eva here could eat the south end of a northbound horse, couldn't you, gal?"

Eva nodded. She was too tired to speak and, as she saw Jubal leave, she shuddered to think that she would be alone with Uncle Fergus. She wished, then, that he would just kill her. She was too tired to resist. She wished she were back home with her mother. She wished they had never left the Savage ranch.

But most of all, she wished John Savage would come through the door and shoot Fergus dead.

Then she wished John would take her in his arms and hold her until she woke up from this nightmare.

9

BOBBITT FREIGHT LINES HAD AN OFFICE AND DEPOT AT THE END
of Curtis Street in downtown Denver. There was a large false
front where the office was located. Next door was a loading
platform and storehouse. There was another warehouse ad-
jacent, and in back, there was a large corral and livery stable next to a shed where wagons could be stored.

Earl Bobbitt was an energetic man with a florid face
framed by snowy whiskers and flaring sideburns. He wore
blue suspenders that held up serge trousers. He wore a
linsey-woolsey shirt dyed a pale blue and leather lace-up
shoes. His wife, Anella, was a buxom woman in her forties
who acted as dispatcher and accountant while Earl handled
sales and orders and helped Anella with schedules. Their
two sons, Phillip and Jerome, worked as loaders and tended
to the horses and wagons.

It was a family business.

Earl had acquired a great deal of wealth since the end of
the Civil War, buying up U.S. Army wagons at cheap prices

and acquiring horses. He drove the first freight wagon himself, from Denver to Cheyenne, and gradually expanded his business. He did not trust banks and kept his money in a large safe at home. He never carried more than ten dollars in his pocket. He paid his sons and his drovers salaries, but paid none to his wife or himself. This was a source of constant quarreling between man and wife.

"You can't trust banks, and I give you an allowance, Anella. What would you need a salary for?" he would say.

"For my own self-respect," she would reply.

"That's something you have to work out for yourself. I respect you. It doesn't take a salary for you to respect yourself."

"Yes. You pay the boys. Why don't you pay me?"

"What's mine is yours, Anella. Giving you a salary would just be a waste of money. You'd spend it on frivolous things, things you don't need."

"It would be my money to spend as I wished. I feel like a prisoner. I never see the money after you take it home and hide it in the safe."

"Then you have nothing to worry about, my dear. The money is safe and when I die, it will all be yours."

"Humph," she snorted. "Fat lot of good that would do me. I'd be so old myself all I'd get to buy would be a wheelchair."

"Let it be," he always said. "I provide for you, and that should be enough."

"Oh, I hope you die before you reach fifty, Earl, you stingy old goat."

The conversations between them at night when he carried the day's receipts home were all pretty much the same. Then they would have tea, she would fix supper, and the boys would sit at the table with them just like any normal, happy family.

Neither Earl nor Anella was aware that two men had been watching them for the past two weeks. Nor were their sons conscious of being watched as they loaded and unloaded wagons or tended to the horses and greased the wagons.

Fred Craven sat inside the little cantina across the street, sipping from a cool glass of *tepache*, a mild alcoholic drink made from a mixture of beer and fruit by Leonora Sanchez, the owner. As Fred told Dick Everson, his partner, "You can drink it all day and never get drunk."

The two men stayed in a boardinghouse next to the cantina, where they had a good view of the freight office. Dick usually stayed in the room or walked to the back lot of Bobbitt's to look at the horses and watch the boys as they painted wagons or shoed their horses. He admired them for their industriousness because they did things he had never done and vowed he never would. He smoked his cheroot, and nobody paid him much attention because he looked like any other bum who roamed the Denver streets looking for handouts.

Fred puffed on a cheroot and waited for Dick. They would always meet at the end of the day when Bobbitt closed up his office and the family piled into a tarp-top buggy and rode out to their home in Cherry Hills. The two had followed them home many times. Fred even climbed a tree so he could see into Bobbitt's bedroom. He watched Bobbitt empty all the money out of the strongbox and put it in the safe. At night, in their room at Mabe's Boardinghouse, they compared notes and wrote down times that might be important to Fergus Blanchett when the time came.

Any day now, Fred thought. He blew a thin plume of blue smoke from his mouth and set the cheroot in a clay *cenicero*. Next to the cantina was a little Mexican shop that sold small gifts, *regales*, and groceries. The sign outside the open air shop just read ABARROTES, and Fred didn't know what it meant.

Mrs. Sanchez made the *tepache* in a large olla that she covered with cheesecloth while it fermented during the night. The drink was always fresh each morning, and she always had a smile for her most persistent customer.

"You want more *tepache*?" she asked as she whisked by on her way out to visit with her friend next door. She always did that just before the little sundries shop closed in late afternoon. Mrs. Sanchez would serve drinks until midnight when the cantina would be filled with Mexicans who worked in the beet fields or picked cherries out on North Federal. They would stream in after dark, dirty and thirsty, and she would have a band of musicians on the stage all tuned up to play the sad songs of their homeland south of the border, the *son huastecos* and the gay songs of Sonora and Jalisco, with trumpets and drums, fiddles and guitars in all sizes.

"No. This will do it for me, Mrs. Sanchez," Fred said, and she waddled onto the dirt street and disappeared.

She trusts me, he thought, and picked up the cheroot for the last few puffs. *She isn't scared that I'll rob her or anything. In other times, I might have. But not now. She doesn't know me, but she trusts me. That's something. That's really something.*

Fred wore a black raincoat much of the time. It concealed the .45 on his hip, and he liked the way he looked in it. He kept his black moustache neatly trimmed and never let his sideburns grow too long. He took his clothes to a Chinese laundry because he liked his shirts to be smooth and pressed and a crease in his dark gabardine trousers. He polished his own boots and dabbed his face with lilac water after he shaved. Fergus called him a dandy, but he resented the term.

"I just like to look good. And when I look good, I feel good," he'd say to Fergus.

"You smell like a damned whorehouse," Fergus would say, but it was all just good-natured joking to Fred's mind.

Fred could feel the sun going down. Shadows began to crawl up the buildings across the street and darken the windows. He put out the stub of his cheroot and started looking for Dick to pass by after making his rounds out in back of Bobbitt's. He finished the last of the *tepache* and felt the glow it gave him, tasted its sweetness and the tiny bites of the beer on his tongue.

Across the street he saw Mrs. Bobbitt light a lamp on her desk.

Still at work, Fred thought. *Makin' all that money and cartin' it home. Well, ain't you fat and sassy, Mrs. Bobbitt.* He smiled at his ruminations and smoothed his moustache.

The Bobbitt boys came around the corner in their fancy buggy with its fringed top and tassels. He knew their names by then—Phil and Jerry. Phil was the older boy, probably about twenty-one, and Jerry was no more than eighteen, he figured. Nice boys. Hard workers, so Dick had told him. They didn't look like any of the boys he had grown up with back in Tennessee. Them boys, he thought, were tough as hickory and still had the bark on when they grew into men. These boys were soft and clean-shaved, like Sunday school boys.

The lamp went out, and Fred saw Earl Bobbitt and Anella walk outside. Earl carried his cash box under his arm and let Anella lock the door.

She never carries the money, Fred mused silently. *He always carries that strongbox and won't let nobody touch it.*

Earl and Anella climbed into the one-horse buggy and settled in the back seat. Phil let off the brake and snapped the reins over the roan gelding's back. The buggy lurched forward, snapping Earl and Anella back against their seat.

Fred watched the buggy until it disappeared down the street, passing all the Mexicans who lived and worked on Curtis. The street darkened just as Dick walked around the corner of the warehouse and passed the loading dock.

Dick crossed the street, and Fred walked out of the cantina to meet him.

"We goin' to foller them home again?" Dick asked.

"No need. We got what we want."

"So, is Fergus back yet?"

"I don't know. He said to keep checking at the Larimer."

"Warn't there last night."

"No. But maybe he'll be there tonight. 'Sides, we can hit a saloon or two, spark some with the glitter gals, and eat steak for supper instead of frijoles and tortillas."

"I'm for that, Fred. I'm plumb tuckered and my eyes feel like they been in a dart game."

"Let's saddle up and ride down to the Larimer. Liveliest street in Denver."

Dick, wearing a nondescript gray shirt and brown pants, a worn leather vest, and dusty boots, fell in alongside Fred as they walked to the stable where their horses were boarded.

"Anything new?" Fred asked.

"Same old routine, Fred. Wagons comin' in and goin' out, Loading and unloading. Jerry shoed a horse. Phil painted a wagon tongue. Jesus, this job is boring."

"Won't last much longer, I'm thinkin'."

"I'm just glad as hell it's night almost. Spyin' on folks is pure drudge work, you ask me."

The two men passed Mrs. Sanchez, who smiled and waved cheerily as she scurried back to her cantina. The clouds overhead turned gray and the night crept into the

town. Lights blinked on in the taverns and saloons, the cantinas and the dance halls. A lone streetlamp burned farther
down Curtis Street.

From some distant unseen point a trumpet rollicked up
the scale from a low C to a high E, and then sounded a trilling arpeggio that seemed to harken another Denver night
with laughter and song.

But all Fred could think about was that strongbox under
Earl Bobbitt's arm and all the times he had seen him carry
it home and bring it back to his office empty every morning.
The thought matched the sweet taste lingering in his mouth
from the cool *tepache*.

And, soon, he thought, *no more Mrs. Sanchez and her
bright smile in that wrinkled face.*

No more Denver.

No more spying on the Bobbitt family.

Fred pulled a pair of cheroots from his pocket and of-
fered one to Dick.

Dick took it, and Fred fished out a match from his pocket,
struck it on his boot heel. He lit the little cigars and they
continued on their way, trailing plumes of smoke, the glow
from their cheroots like a pair of fireflies performing aerial
acrobatics as the darkness settled like a black shroud over
the two men.

10

BENITO LIFTED DIRT OUT OF THE GROUND WITH HIS SHOVEL. AT the other end of the grave, Gasparo was loosening the soil. Nearby, amid the pines, was the grave of young Whit Blanchett, Emma's son, who had hanged himself. Sunlight flickered through pine boughs or streamed in slanted columns all around the two men. Sweat soaked through their shirts and they wiped the sweatbands of their hats every few minutes and swiped their faces with sodden kerchiefs.

Gasparo stopped digging and looked across the creek toward the road that led into the large pasture. A few of the cattle raised their heads and looked in that same direction.

"You hear that, Benito?"

Benito placed both hands on the handle of his shovel and turned his head.

"I think a wagon is coming."

"Ah, finally, Carlos, he comes."

Benito shaded his eyes and stared at the road where it came into the field.

"Yes," he said, "Carlos comes. I hope he brings the *aguardiente*."

"And maybe some bottles of tequila or mescal."

"Something to make our brains rot when the sun falls behind the mountains."

"We will have a cup for Juanito, eh? The three of us."

The wagon hove into view, topping the rise. To their surprise, the driver turned the team so that he was headed toward them.

"That is not Carlos," Gasparo said. "And, the wagon is pulling the horse of Juanito."

"You are right, Gasparo. That is not Carlos."

"It is Ben," Gasparo said as the wagon rumbled toward them.

"Where is Carlos?" Benito said. "I do not see him."

"Maybe he is in the jail."

"Do they have a jail in Butterfly Creek?"

"I do not know," Gasparo said.

The wagon drew closer. Cows moved out of its way and some of them bellowed at the intrusion.

"I do not want to know," Benito said, trying to make a little joke, because he had an odd feeling that something was wrong. Ben should not be driving the supply wagon back. And where was John? No, something was not right, but he did not say anything to Gasparo. Instead, he looked at him and saw that there was worry on his face, the way his eyes squinted amidst a very somber expression. He looked down at the body of Juanito, wrapped in a blanket like an Egyptian mummy, and he felt a queasiness in his stomach, as if the coffee he had drunk was turning as sour as stale vinegar.

Blue jays flitted among the branches, hurling staccato invective at the diggers. Squirrels and chipmunks scratched among the fallen and decaying pine needles. A pair of crows sailed through the timber, chased by jays and sparrows. The wagon rumbled to a full stop by the creek. Ben set the brake with a screech louder than the jays. The crows cawed as they fluttered away, trailing a host of gyrating birds.

"*Hola*, Ben," Gasparo called.

Ben jumped down from the wagon, tossing the reins down, which rattled like birdshot on the wood.

"Need a hand, boys," he called. "And I'm in a hurry."

Benito and Gasparo let their shovels drop and ran to the creek. They waded across water up to their knees and slogged to the opposite bank. Ben walked to the rear of the wagon and dropped the tailgate.

"What you got?" Gasparo asked as he sopped up to Ben.

"Carlos," Ben said.

"He does not move. Is he asleep?"

"He's dead, Gasparo. You and Benito have to bury him."

"*Dios mio*. Carlos is dead?"

"He does not move," Benito said, craning his neck to look at the rigid body in the wagon bed. "The flies, they eat him."

Gasparo swore under his breath.

The fluting call of a mountain quail sounded oddly out of place in the solemnity of the moment. Benito and Gasparo seemed unable to move as they both stared at the remains of Carlos Montoya.

Ben untied the rope from Cholo's bridle. He threw it in the wagon.

"I'm going to switch horses. You boys take care of Carlos and get these goods unloaded."

"Where do you go, Ben?" Gasparo asked.

"John rode down to that creek town. He's hunting the man who did this to Juanito and Carlos."

"You will kill this man?" Benito asked.

"Killing him would be too merciful," Ben said. He

climbed into the saddle. "I hate to leave him like this, but I've got to go help John."

"You will ride Thunder," Benito said.

"Yes. You can rub Cholo down when you get finished with the unloading and the burials. I'm sorry, boys. It just has to be this way."

"Yes," Gasparo said. "We will put a clean shirt on Carlos and wash him and he will be buried next to Juanito."

Ben touched a finger to the brim of his hat and rode off toward the barn and stables. He felt guilty about leaving Carlos to be buried by Benito and Gasparo. He hoped they would understand that he had more urgent matters on his mind. There was no telling what John was riding into, and even if he could find the killer of his two hands, he might not be able to handle it alone.

He unsaddled Cholo and put his own saddle and bridle on his horse, Thunder. He got his own rifle and stuffed cartridges in his pockets and put an extra box in his saddlebags. He put the food Ornery had prepared in his saddlebags, as well. Ornery came out of the cook shack, and Ben told him what had happened, what the boys were doing.

"So, I got groceries," Ornery said.

"You do. I expect they'll bring the wagon up once they get over the shock of seeing Carlos like that."

"You say his throat was cut, too?"

"Same as Juanito."

"Bastard," Ornery said.

"Don't know when we'll be back," Ben said, as he climbed into the saddle and turned his horse in a tight circle.

"Maybe I ought to strap on my own Colt."

"Wouldn't hurt."

"That's a hell of a note, Ben."

"Ain't it though?"

Ben rode off through the pasture. He saw the wagon pull away from the creek and head for the stables. Benito and Gasparo waved at him and he waved back. He rode with a heavy heart, thinking of the two men who had died with such heartless savagery, both innocent of any wrongdoing. They were both just in the wrong place at the wrong time. No, that wasn't right. They were hunted down by some bastard who lusted after a woman, thinking she was claimed by John.

Senseless, he thought. No woman was worth the life of even one man, much less two.

He put the spurs to Thunder and rode him a quarter mile at a gallop, then slowed him to a walk.

He rubbed the horse's neck, patted him. He didn't want Thunder to sweat in the heat, but he was damned sure in a hurry to get to Butterfly Creek, which had no business being where it was, on their creek, the same creek he and John had panned for gold, defended with their lives, and seen its waters run with the blood of their friends and families.

Ben rode into the clapboard town that had sprung up along the creek. Like so many others, it had no design, was not plotted nor planned, but was just a jumble of shacks made from whipsawed lumber and ten-penny nails, an assemblage of hotels, saloons, and shacks sprawled on both sides of the creek. A sawmill up in the timber ate trees like some voracious beast, chewing the pines into boards and providing sawdust for taverns and fireplaces. Smoke rose from a half dozen crude chimneys made of tin. Prospectors panned and sluiced the creek while others dug and blasted. Mules strapped to long poles worked the *arrastres* that ground the rock into chunks and powder. The air was filled with soot and dust and the noise of industry as people crawled like ants looking for gold in the form of nuggets or dust, while the merchants grabbed coin and paper money as fast as it was minted.

He rode to Emma's house, his nostrils filled with the stench and odor of human sweat, smoke from coal or oil fires, beef frying on stoves, biscuits and bread baking in ovens, tortillas on *hornos*, human and animal waste teeming with flies and vermin.

He saw the note on Emma's door, dismounted, and snatched it with his hand. He read it quickly and murmured the words: "Larimer Hotel in Denver. Meet you there, Ben."

"Shit," he said and walked back to his horse, crumpling the note into a ball that he tossed in the dirt.

The day was burning away in the hot spring sun, and he had a long, two-day ride ahead of him. He grabbed a sandwich from his saddlebag and munched it on the way down to the flat, through the stunted pines, the cactus and sagebrush, pulling on his canteen between bites, with Thunder's hooves ringing on stone and the sound of the sawmill's buzz in his ears.

He patted his horse's head, pulled his boots from the stirrups and stretched his legs, wriggled his toes.

"I'm gettin' too damned old for this, Thunder," he said. "And you ain't gettin' no younger, either."

Thunder snorted and tossed his head as if he understood.

The sun burned through Ben's shirt and blistered the back of his neck. His hands turned red, and sweat oozed from his pores until his shirt stiffened with salt that acted like starch, turning the cloth stiff as it dried in the breeze.

He wished that he and John had never met Emma and her daughter, Eva.

"A woman ain't nothin' but trouble, Thunder," he said.

But he knew that wasn't true. Man was trouble, with his greed and avarice, his insatiable appetite for gold. And he and John were among them, driven by some unknown force to plunder the earth just to satisfy that same hunger that was as natural to man as breathing the air.

Ben was getting old, but sometimes, when he was feeling like he was this day, he thought he might have been born old.

He could no longer remember ever being young.

11

JOHN WAS SURPRISED WHEN EMMA CHANGED INTO A PAIR OF black trousers and strapped on a gunbelt with a Smith & Wesson .38-caliber revolver in the holster. She wore a blue chambray shirt and a flat-crowned hat. In the saddle, he might have taken her for a man.

When she stepped out from the clump of trees and sagebrush with her dress and shoes under her arm, John almost did not recognize her. They had stopped at her request a few miles from the creek so that she could change clothes.

"In some parts of the country, you'd be horsewhipped for wearing pants," he said.

"That's why I pack a .38," she said, a mischievous smile on her face.

"I hope you know how to use it."

"My aim is pretty good."

"I'll bet it is." He smiled at her as she stuffed her clothes and shoes into her saddlebag.

"Ready to ride, John? If your eyes bulge out any more, they're going to get sunburned."

She climbed onto her horse and clucked to it as she reined it to turn toward John.

"The only woman I ever saw who wore pants was my aunt Bertha," he said. "She smoked cigars, too."

Emma laughed as she pulled up alongside him.

"Did she carry a pistol?" she asked.

"Not like you do. Hers you couldn't see. She wore a real small .22 tucked inside her belt."

"I want people who don't like women wearing pants to see my pistol. It discourages comment or horsewhipping."

He laughed, and they rode down out of the hills and onto the flat.

John did not see the horse tracks he was looking for on the road. He didn't know exactly where Fergus might have left the foothills, but he knew if Fergus and his companion were heading for Denver this was the only road. He and Emma rode in silence for about two miles while he scanned the road. There were tracks, wagon and horse, but not the distinctive ones he was looking for.

"You stay on the road, Emma. I'm going to range on both sides to see if I can pick up any tracks from Fergus's horse."

"If he was going to Denver, wouldn't he take this road?"

"Yes, but if he didn't want anybody to see him with your daughter, he might just go overland."

"I see," she said.

"If he, or the man he may be riding with, is carrying your daughter, I'll be able to tell. If she is riding a separate horse, I'll know that, too."

"Just from the tracks?"

"Just from the tracks."

He turned Gent off the road to the left and rode back and

forth across a wide swath, studying the ground for the faintest sign that horses had passed. It was slow work and Emma kept pace with him, stopping her horse every so often so that she would not lose sight of him.

He shook his head and rode back to where Emma was waiting.

"I'll try the other side of the road."

"Nothing over there?"

"No."

A Mexican driving a wagon loaded with woven serapes and blankets passed them from the south. He waved as he went by, driving his two burros. They saw no other riders.

John worked the right side of the road, ranging fifty to two hundred yards. It did not take long for him to find tracks about a hundred yards parallel. He saw the trampled brush and the displaced stones, the crushed cactus blossoms and mangled prairie flowers, and in the open places, the marks of iron hooves.

He stopped Gent and climbed out of the saddle to study the tracks of two horses. One was made by Fergus's horse, with the heel stud broken off and the worn spot on one side. The other horse sank its hooves deeper into the soft sand. He knew that Eva was probably riding with that man. The extra weight would explain the deep impressions.

When he was satisfied, he returned to the road where Emma was waiting, her horse switching its tail at flies and biting the ones that were attacking shoulders and sides.

"Well?" she said.

"They're heading for Denver, all right. Fergus and another man. That man is undoubtedly carrying Eva with him."

"Oh, the beast," she said.

"They'll have to stop for the night. But I see no use in following their tracks. It will slow us down."

"To think that Eva will have to spend the night with that bastard . . ."

"They probably won't sleep more than a couple of hours. We'll have to stop and rest ourselves."

"Yes, I'm sure."

"Emma," he said, "don't worry about things you can't change. We'll find Eva in Denver. We'll get her back."

"I wish I had your confidence in that, John."

"We know where Fergus will be. And where he is, Eva will be. That's all we need to know at this point."

"Then we'd best keep riding toward Denver," she said.

He saw the determination in her face, but he also saw the worry in her blue eyes. He was grateful that she wasn't a hysterical woman. He admired her not only for her grit but for her control over her emotions. As a mother, he knew she must be torn apart inside, wondering what those men might do to Eva, and wondering if she would ever see her daughter alive again. He wondered if her imagination was akin to his, because he thought of all the terrible things that could befall a young woman like Eva in the hands of two merciless killers like Fergus and his sidekick. He hoped she was not that imaginative and that she was just hoping to get her daughter away from a man she obviously hated.

He knew there must be more to Emma's story than she had told him. More to Fergus himself than she had let on.

Emma, he knew, was carrying a lot of weight, and it wasn't all about her daughter.

Doves whistled past them as they rode, twisting in the air like gray ballerinas in flight, and they saw quail cross the road in single file, fat little children in feathers following their teacher. In the distance, far out on the prairie, buzzards swung in circles, floating on air currents none could see, their wings spread wide to pick up every slight shift of air, and some dropped from the sky, their wings folded until they opened them to cushion their landings.

The sun inched across the blue sky flocked with white clouds, and they could see the snowy peaks of the Rockies glistening, throwing off billions of bright sparks that would blind a man at close range. The mountains looked eternal in the distance, dominating the land, their muscled bulks of rock and dirt forming a barrier between prairie and distant sea.

Still, they rode on. They drank from their canteens and seldom spoke. John was hungry, but he did not want to stop to take the time to eat. He wanted to make at least twenty miles or more, if they could, before they stopped for the night. He set the pace with Gent, and Emma kept up with him. He put the horse into a trot every so often, and a few times they galloped, the wind from their speed cooling them off in the blaze of sun. Once or twice, Emma laughed when he slowed Gent and put him once again to a walk.

"You like to ride fast," he said.

"It brings back good memories," she said. "Before, when I was a child in Tennessee, we used to race our horses on Sunday picnics and at pie socials, the summer get-togethers with other families and relatives."

"You went to pie socials," he said.

Emma blushed and she gave him a sly look.

"I bake a pretty good pie, John."

"I know. I've tasted them. Only thing is, I didn't pay to share it with you."

"Oh, the boys paid, all right," she said. "And they wanted more than pie."

"And did you give it to them?"

She blushed again and it gave her face a radiant look. He thought that she looked so natural on her horse, so unlike any woman he'd known besides his mother.

"No, you silly. I was a very proper young lady, I'll have you know."

"I never doubted it. You're a proper lady now, in fact."

"Oh, you flatter me, John Savage."

But she was pleased at the compliment, he knew. She wore it like a dainty shawl on her shoulders. She seemed to grow more beautiful with every mile they rode together, and he was feeling things in his heart, faint stirrings that were new to him, new and full of energy and promise.

They watched the sun dip slowly behind the snowcapped mountains and felt a change in the air temperature.

"Hungry?" she asked as they watched the shadows of their horses elongate and stretch into lumpy specters to the east, the plants alongside dull in the fading light.

"Fairly," he said. "We'll stop for the night sometime after the sun goes down."

"I'll ride as long as you want," she said. "Every mile brings us closer to where Eva is."

He nodded and put spurs to Gent. They rode at a brisk spurt for a quarter of a mile before he slowed his horse to a walk. Gent seemed to want to run out from under him, and John patted him on the withers to show that he understood.

The sun disappeared behind the mountains, leaving a majestic painting in the sky, the white clouds burnished with gold and silver, the empty spaces shimmering with showers of brilliant light. Then the colors faded to purples and grays and the light shrunk, the golden shafts dissolving into ashen clouds that proclaimed the solemn dusk and the hush that fell over the hills and the prairie.

John had been looking for a place to spend the night, and he saw a small canyon off to his left. He turned Gent and beckoned for Emma to follow him.

"Are we going in there?" she asked, standing up in her stirrups to look over her horse's head.

"We can build a fire there against the rocks and be out of the wind," he said.

"Looks like a good place." She settled back down in her saddle.

It was nearly full dark when they entered the small canyon, which was almost as narrow as an arroyo out on the plain. They stopped and dismounted, deep in shadows.

"Do we unsaddle our horses, John?"

"No. Just hobble them. There's not much graze here, but we won't stay all night."

"It's getting cold," she said.

"I'll make us a fire quick as I can. We'll lay out our bedrolls next to that slab of rock where I'm going to put the fire."

They both gathered brush and broken limbs that had fallen or been washed into the defile, and John lit a match and started a small fire. They laid out their bedrolls between the fire and the rock face. Emma brought out their food. They sat by the fire and ate, washing down their food with water from their canteens.

Somewhere out on the prairie, a coyote called, and there was an answering chorus of yips and yelps.

"I love it here," she said softly as she took off her hat and lay down on her bedroll. "No dishes to wash, no table to clear. I could live like this forever."

He lay down beside her on his own bedroll.

"The country gets to you," he said. "It gets inside you, and you learn who you really are."

"Yes," she breathed and pulled her blanket over her.

He put more wood on the fire and saw that Emma had fallen asleep.

He crawled under his own blanket and took off his hat.

Orange light splayed across her face and shadows danced

on her closed eyes, the curves of her body, as she slept next to him.

John gazed up at the stars shining so brightly above him, seeming so close he could reach up and grab them like diamonds out of the sky. His eyelids grew heavy and he drifted off to sleep, the scent of Emma like some dreamy aroma from a special place known only to gods and goddesses wafting over him as she slept next to him.

12

THE DIAMONDBACK RATTLER SLITHERED UNDER EMMA'S blanket. It crawled up over her boot and into the leg of her trousers. It burrowed clear to her inner thigh. Emma felt something crawling there. She woke up and slapped at the lump inside her pants. The rattlesnake sank its fangs into the soft flesh, injecting two squirts of venom through the punctures.

Emma screamed and bolted out of her bedroll, slapping at the squirming snake. It released its grip and fell out of her pants just as John woke up and saw Emma standing there in the fire glow, screaming at the top of her lungs. He saw the snake fall to the ground and heard its rattle as it zig-zagged away from her.

He jumped up and grabbed Emma.

"Were you bit?" he asked.

"It—it stung me," she screamed. "What was it?"

"A rattlesnake," he said. "Where did it bite you?"

She pointed to her leg and began to whimper.

"It hurts," she said.

"Quick," he said. "Lie down and don't move. Breathe real slow."

She lay down. John put more sticks on the fire. He knelt beside her.

"I'm going to take off your boots and pants. Lie real still, Emma."

"My pants?" She was trembling.

"I've got to get that poison out."

She whimpered deep inside her throat.

John pulled off her boots. Then he pulled her trousers down, slipped them off, and set them aside.

He leaned over close enough to see the two punctures in her skin. A yellowish substance like pus oozed from the twin holes. They were on her inner leg just below her panties. He drew his knife and held the blade over the fire.

"What are you doing?" she murmured.

"Making the blade sterile."

He brought the knife close to her.

"This is going to hurt," he said. "Grit your teeth."

John sliced two small crosses over the puncture holes. Venom pushed out from both new wounds. He bent down and placed his mouth over one cross and sucked the poison out. He spit the deadly fluid out and sucked the other cross. He spit that out and continued to suck at both holes until he was drawing only a small amount of blood. Emma moaned and squirmed, but kept her left leg still. He took off his bandanna and tied it around her leg above the fang bites. He reached down and picked up a stick, tied a knot around it with the bandanna and twisted the stick until it was tight.

"This will hurt for a while," he said. "Until I loosen it. But it will keep any venom left from getting up your bloodstream and into your heart."

"Ummm," Emma moaned, clamping her teeth tightly.

"Leave your pants off. I'll loosen the tourniquet after a while and then tighten it again."

"Am I going to die?" she said.

"I think we got the worst of it out quick enough. You may get a little sick, but you won't die."

"It doesn't hurt so much. Not like it did. Only that bandanna."

"Just try to relax and lie real still."

"I will," she said and let out a long sigh as she lay her head down and looked up at him.

"I'll sit with you, Emma." He took her hand in his and held it, squeezing it gently.

"Thank you, John," she breathed and closed her eyes.

He looked at her face in the flickering firelight. He saw the dark shapes of bats just overhead. They dove into the darkness at the end of the canyon and whisked by again, twisting in the air, their leathery wings fanning his face. He could hear their tiny squeaks as they flew by, scooping up airborne insects.

Later, he loosened the makeshift tourniquet and rubbed the depression in her skin. He tied it again, but not so tightly. He looked for blue streaks going up her leg, but saw none.

"I feel sick to my stomach," she said.

"That's probably just shock from the snakebite, Emma. Just breathe regular and don't move your sore leg."

"All right."

"I don't think the poison is getting into your veins. The snake didn't pump too much venom when it bit you."

"That's a relief."

He touched her forehead, and it was damp with sweat. She had no fever, and that was a good sign, he thought.

"Close your eyes," he said. "Try to sleep if you can."

"Yes. Very tired." Her voice was barely audible.

He added more fuel to the fire and watched her, looking

for any sign that the venom might have reached her heart. Her breathing was shallow but even. She looked so beautiful in the fire's orange glow, her features chiseled out of alabaster or marble. Her lips were slightly parted and her hair glistened as shadows danced across her face and head. He continued to hold her hand in his.

Sometimes, he knew, a rattlesnake that was driven off from its prey would sneak back. He kept looking for any sign of the rattler, his ears attuned to every small sound. But he saw nothing and heard nothing for the next half hour or so. He released her hand and touched the cuts and holes in her leg. There was no more bleeding, and the wounds seemed to be dry.

With gentle fingers, John untied the bandanna and removed the small stick. He bent down to see if there were any lines above the place where the tourniquet had been. Her skin looked smooth and unblemished. There was no sign that the venom was coursing through her bloodstream.

He breathed a sigh of relief and rubbed her leg beneath the wrinkled place where the bandanna had been. He rubbed her flesh down to the crosses to see if any more venom or blood oozed out of either hole. He was relieved to see that the wounds were closing up and not leaking any fluids.

Emma slept as John watched over her.

He put more wood on the fire as the stars wheeled in the night sky. He saw that the Big Dipper had moved as had the other constellations.

We are so small here, he thought. *Like the wind, life is so short the universe hardly notices it.* Yet life has its intense moments, and this was one of them. Death had passed Emma by, but as the leaves died and tumbled in autumn, death came and went, taking old life away and somehow bringing new life into existence. The leaves that appeared on the trees in spring were not the same leaves as those that had turned brown and fallen away, but they carried the memories of those leaves that had once adorned the trees.

John stretched over Emma and reached for his pistol that was rolled up in his gunbelt next to where his head had lain. He had heard a rustle in the sandy floor of the canyon. It might have been his imagination or a small animal, a rat or a rabbit. He unwrapped his gunbelt and slid his pistol from its holster. He held it in his hand, his thumb on the cross-hatched hammer.

He scooted around to face the place where he thought he had heard the soft grating of sand. He peered into the flick-ering shadows beyond the firelight. He sat very still and listened with a heightened sensitivity. He held his breath for long periods and let it out very slowly.

Some small movement caught his eye. He stared at an emptiness, holding very still, breathing very slowly.

A small section of ground seemed to move. He wanted to rub his eyes to see if they were working right. He saw nothing tangible, but he wondered if something had moved. There had been a small shift in the sand, and that wasn't normal. He continued to stare at the spot where he thought he had seen movement.

His eyes began to burn. His ears seemed empty of all sound.

Then he heard a soft grating sound and saw the sand undulate, curving away from something that he could not see.

But he knew what it was.

The rattlesnake had returned and was slithering along the opposite wall of the canyon. He waited, watching that portion of sand that he could still see, sand that was still flat and undisturbed.

His ears began to ache slightly from the strain of listen-ing for the tiniest of sounds. His eyes were blistered inside from the strain of staring at shadows and bare patches of sand and the small lumps of rocks and pebbles.

Then, there it was again, that small sound of sand shifting. He saw the pattern then, the dark geometric patches of scales, the ripple of a snake's body inching toward him, no longer parallel to the wall.

He watched the snake's body curve and slide over the sandy floor of the canyon. It moved faster than before. He could just barely see its head, and in the orange glow of the fire, he thought he saw its black forked tongue flitting in and out of its hideous mouth.

John raised his pistol from his lap. He swung the barrel toward the snake.

The rattlesnake stopped for a moment and lifted its head to seek him out with its nervous tongue.

Then it bunched its scales and slid even closer.

John cocked the pistol. The lock made a metallic snick as the hammer came to full cock.

The snake rippled into a coil and raised its head and its tail.

Then its tail shook back and forth, setting off the ominous clatter of rattles that sounded like a leather box full of clacking dice.

A rattle that was like the guttural rasp of death itself.

It was coiled to strike. It drew its head back, and its tongue flicked in and out of its mouth in rapid succession like a bolt of ebony lightning.

John's finger touched the curve of the Colt's trigger as he held his breath and his eyes bored into that single image of the snake's head coiling back toward its rattling tail.

13

FERGUS BLANCHETT STUDIED EVA'S FACE AS SHE SAT ON THE small divan. She felt his scouring gaze as if he had her pinned with the skewers of his eyes. He did not look at anything but her face, and she wondered if her skin was still red from his slaps. She had the feeling that he was about to explode in a sudden rage and maybe kill her.

"You got your grandma's eyes," he said, his voice low and guttural. "Her nose, too. And maybe her lips."

"I—I never knew your mother," she said, her voice weak and full of timidity.

"No, she was dead when you was borned."

Eva trembled inside. She was afraid of this man. He looked like her father, whose image had been fading from her mind so that it was hard to picture him. But her uncle Fergus looked enough like him that she suddenly remembered her father, who had that same intensity in his eyes when he was angry at her mother. Brown eyes that turned black and impenetrable when he was mad at something.

"You coulda been my kid," Fergus said. "Damn your ma."

Eva flinched at his words. She didn't know what he was talking about.

Without any warning, he walked over to the wardrobe that was standing against the wall. He opened both doors. It was empty except for pegs near the top on which to hang clothing.

Eva shrank back as he turned and walked toward her.

"Get up and get in there," he growled.

"Huh?"

"You heard me. Get inside that wardrobe and sit down. And shut up."

She trembled all over as she got to her feet. She walked to the wardrobe and hesitated.

"Why?" she said.

"Damn you. Just get in there and sit down."

"No," she said, shrinking away from the empty wardrobe.

"What are you scared of, Eva? Did your ma ever lock you in the closet?"

"No," she said.

"How about your pa?"

She shook her head, but her lips quivered in fear. Her father had locked her in the woodshed when she was naughty, and she knew his father had done the same to him. She had been terrified when he'd closed the door and padlocked it. She suffered a smothering feeling when she was in dark, enclosed places. When she was very little, she remembered the terror of those times when she was afraid of snakes and rats and would hear strange sounds until he let her out.

"You're a damned liar," he said. He pushed her inside the wardrobe. She slammed into the wall and crumpled, her legs quivering as she squatted.

Fergus closed both doors, and she heard him doing something to the knobs.

"You stay quiet, gal, hear?"

Eva began sobbing. She heard his boots clomp on the floor as he moved away. She sat down and put her head on her knees, holding them tight against her. It was dark inside, with only a few lines of weak lamplight glimmering through the slight crack in the doors. Her pulse hammered in her ears. She could feel her heart thump in her chest. She closed her eyes and tried to calm down while her mind raced with thoughts of being imprisoned in the woodshed and, sometimes, back east, the storm cellar.

Jubal let himself back in the room with his key. He carried a basket of hot food over to the table.

"Where's the girl?" he asked as he set the wicker basket on the small table. "I got enough food for all three of us."

"She ain't eatin'," Fergus said.

Jubal pulled the cloth from the top of the basket and took out a bottle of Old Taylor and two glasses.

"I got to take the basket and water glasses back," he said.

"We get to keep the napkins?" Fergus asked, a sarcastic twang to his voice.

"No, them, too."

The two men sat down at the table. Fergus poured whiskey in both glasses, while Jubal set out plates of tamales, beans, rice, and fried apples.

"They said they'd wash the plates. I give 'em a deposit."

The two men drank and ate voraciously. Eva could hear them chomping on their food, and her stomach churned with hunger.

Uncle Fergus is so cruel, she thought. She was starving and he was probably eating like a pig.

She tried to think of something else, and her thoughts drifted to her mother and to John Savage. They never should have left the ranch; she knew that. If they had stayed, John could have protected them. She hoped he would come to her rescue. She hoped that he would beat up her uncle. No, that was not enough. He had that gun with all the silver words on the barrel. He should shoot Fergus. Shoot him down like a dog. Her stomach growled, and then all she could think about was food and her mother's cooking.

There were loud knocks on the door.

"See who it is, Jubal," Fergus said, with a mouthful of food.

Eva heard Jubal's heavy boots pounding on the rug and then the soft creak of the door as he opened it.

"Come on in, boys," Jubal said, and Eva heard more footsteps. Her heart beat faster. Maybe, she thought, it was her mother and the wardrobe doors would open and . . .

Her hopes evaporated like soap bubbles blown from a wooden pipe when she heard the gruff voices of two other men.

"Fergus, you goin' to drink all that whiskey by yourself?" Fred Craven said.

"Fred, you touch that bottle and you'll pull back a mangled hand," Fergus said.

"Ain't no need to hog it all," Dick Everson said. "I mean the grub, not the whiskey."

"Dick," Fergus said as he chewed a tough piece of beef, "you can have what scraps is left when me and Jubal finish our grub."

"That's real kind of you, Fergus," Dick said.

"You boys got anything for me?" Fergus asked.

"I got me a powerful thirst, Fergus," Fred said. "That's what I got."

All the men laughed.

"Take a swig, then, and tell me about Bobbitt."

Eva heard the slosh of whiskey as Fred lifted the bottle

to his lips. Every sound in the room was amplified in her dark chamber. She wondered who the two men were who had come into the room and what was a Bobbitt. Was it a man or some term she didn't understand? And then she remembered the wagon she had seen and the legend BOBBITT FREIGHT LINES on the side of it.

"Gimme a taste of that, Fred," Dick said. Fred passed the open bottle to Dick, who swigged down a swallow and smacked his lips.

Eva could smell the food now, and she sniffed at the faint tang of whiskey fumes that drifted into the wardrobe. She thought she might be sick if she didn't get some food in her stomach. But she was intent on listening to what the men had to say and that helped to keep her mind off her hunger.

"Bobbitt had himself a real busy day," Fred said. "I reckon he took in a lot of money."

"They're ripe," Dick said. "Busy week whilst you was gone. And every night he carries that strongbox full of money back to his house."

"We'll wait until they're all fast asleep," Fergus said. His chair scraped on the rug as he got up from the table. "You get them horses, Dick?"

"Yeah, we bought two horses, like you said, and a couple of five-dollar saddles. But I thought you was bringin' your sister-in-law and her kid back to Denver."

"He's got his niece," Jubal said. His spoon scraped against the plate as he scooped up a dollop of beans and rice, stuffed them into his maw.

"Where is she?" Fred asked.

"In that wardrobe there. Didn't want her in the middle of our business. You saddle up one of them horses for her."

"You takin' a kid with us?" Dick asked.

"She won't be no trouble," Fergus said.

Eva thought her ears would burst as she heard her uncle's plan. They were going to do something bad, and they were taking her along. They had bought a horse for her and perhaps another one for her mother. She squeezed her legs and tried to shut down her thoughts. They were all dire.

"What happened with her mother?" Fred asked.

"She'll come. I'll leave her a note at the desk, tellin' her to meet me in Longmont."

"Shit," Dick said. "The sooner you get over your brother's widder woman, the better off you'll be, Fergus."

"You never mind about Emma, Dick. I got plans for her that ain't none of your damned business."

"Sure, sure," Dick said. "Just a heap of trouble, that's all."

"You let me worry about that," Fergus said. "Jubal, take that basket and them dishes and spoons back. We'll head out for Cherry Creek about midnight when them Bobbitts are sound asleep."

"We can sure lighten old Bobbitt's load some," Fred said.

Eva heard the clatter of plates and the tink of spoons falling on them. She was sure now that they were going to rob someone. Someone named Bobbitt. And they were going to take her with them. Perhaps that would give her a chance to run away while they were doing their dirty business. That was some hope, at least. One small hope against the despair she felt.

Jubal stomped across the room.

"Be back in a whistle," he said as he opened the door and left the room.

"I'll saddle one of them horses," Dick said. "We're all set, and I see you and Jubal's horses are at the hitchrail."

"Good," Fergus said. "We'll be set for that midnight ride. I'll write a note for Emma."

"You think she'll ride all the way to Cheyenne?" Fred asked.

"If she wants her daughter back, she'll ride clear to hell," Fergus said.

Eva heard the one called Dick leave the room. Her heart filled with dread. Her stomach muscles tightened as if they were threaded with wire and someone was twisting it tight.

"You think Bobbitt's going to open his safe for us, Fergus?" Fred asked.

"If he wants to spare his wife from gettin' her throat slit, he'll hand over his money like we was holding a collection plate at his church."

"What about them two boys?"

"They'll be the first to go down," Fergus said.

"Then what?"

"What do you think, Fred?"

There was a long pause. Eva strained her ears to hear what Fred would say.

"I think there ain't gonna be no witnesses at the Bobbitt house."

"That's right," Fergus said. "Jim Bowie's knife will see to that."

Then Fergus laughed.

Eva felt the chilled feet of something scaly and amphibious crawl up her spine and she shivered. She had seen the big knife on Fergus's belt, and she knew what a terrible weapon Jim Bowie had wrought before he was killed at the Alamo.

She counted the number of Bobbitts in her mind.

Four people were going to die.

She knew that as sure as she knew her own name.

Eva wanted to scream, but she didn't dare.

14

JOHN SHUT OUT ALL BUT THE SNAKE'S HEAD. THE OPEN MOUTH, the curved white fangs, the jewel-like eyes, the shining scales, all stood out in the firelight, etched on his retinas like a Navajo sand painting under the glare of the noonday sun.

He held his breath like a diver on the high board just before the plunge.

The trigger gave way under the gentle pressure of his finger. He had the distance. He had the snake's head dissected by the blade front sight that was perfectly aligned in the slot of the rear sight.

The .45 exploded in his hand. Flame and orange sparks belched from the barrel. The slug fried the air and smacked into the snake's open mouth, smashing the fangs to bits, blowing off the mangled head in a spray of blood that was like a fine rosy mist in the dazzle of firelight.

John's ears flexed with the concussion even though his mouth was slightly open. He let out his breath as Emma sat up, a loud yell bursting from her throat. The yell became a terrified scream as white smoke spewed from the muzzle of John's pistol, twisting through the air like a ghostly serpent.

He turned to her as the snake's body twisted and thrashed, the rattles fading to a feeble flutter before falling to the ground and ceasing to shake.

"Calm down, Emma."

"It took a long time to die," she said, a tremor in her voice.

"It died as soon as the bullet hit it."

"But it kept moving. And rattling."

"Leftover reflexes is all," he said.

She breathed a soft sigh of relief.

"Can you sleep?" he asked.

"Not after that. No."

"Do you want to rest? The bite hurting you?"

"No. I want to get to Denver. I want my daughter back in my arms. The bite only hurts a little. Not even a hurt. More like a stitch in my leg."

"Emma. I want to know more about Fergus. I think you left some things out. Who did he kill down in Texas?"

"Oh, John, it's all so horrible. So crazy, in a way. There's something wrong with Fergus. And, I think there was a lot wrong with Argus, too."

"What do you mean?"

"Both brothers courted me. I did not like Fergus at all. He was bad blood, pure and simple."

"How do you mean?"

"He got in trouble a lot when he was a kid. Stealing and cruelty, mostly. Argus was pretty bad, too, I guess, but Fergus was far worse. He wanted to marry me. Argus was persistent and I . . . I wanted to get away from home, so I married him. Fergus was furious."

"Understandable," John said.

"But he didn't get over it. He married my sister, Eileen. She was two years older than me."

"What?"

"She was crazy to marry him. She knew what kind of a man he was. But we both wanted to get away from home. We didn't have much love in our house. We were treated like servants. Our parents beat us for the littlest things. They were mean and cruel. We hated them."

"Why? I mean, 'hate' is a pretty strong word."

"They didn't have much and they hated the world, I guess. My mother beat us all the time. She said we were worthless and that my father had to work too hard to support us. They worked us from dawn to dusk and then beat us when we were tired or hungry or too slow."

"So, Fergus married your sister."

"Eileen was a strong young woman. She stood up to our folks. I guess she did the same with Fergus. He killed her. In a fit of rage, they said. He told the court it was an accident. But the truth is he beat her to death. With his fists."

"So, he still wants you."

"He was sentenced to ten years in prison. He must have gotten out early for good behavior."

"Will he hurt Eva?"

"I don't know. He might. Just to get back at me. Oh, John, I'm so worried about her. I want to get her back safe and get far away from Fergus."

"I might have to kill him, Emma."

She leaned forward, her face flushed with emotion, her eyes blazing with a sudden rage.

"Then kill him, John. Kill him. Shoot him dead so I never have to see him again."

"Would you kill him? Could you kill him?"

She sat up straight and her eyes softened.

"If he hurt Eva, yes."

"He's already hurt her. He kidnapped her."

Her face hardened again. Her eyes sparkled in the firelight, a savage blue full of hate and anger.

"I could kill him right now just for doing that," she said. "And you, you have better reasons than I do to kill him."

He took in a breath and nodded.

"Yes. I do have good reason to kill him. But sometimes I question the reasons to kill a man."

"Fergus murdered two of your men. Two of your friends."

"And your sister, Emma."

"I know." She hung her head for a moment as if remembering. "So, you shouldn't question your right to seek vengeance."

"Vengeance," he said. "I wonder if I have the right."

"If anyone does, John, you do."

"My mother would have argued the point, I'm sure."

"Oh, the Bible, you mean. 'Vengeance is mine, sayeth the Lord.'"

"Yes. And conscience."

"But surely you don't think it's wrong to take the life of a killer."

"In some ways, I do, Emma. Who am I to say whether a man should live or die?"

"But you killed my husband. You've killed other men, according to Ben."

"Yes, that's true. I killed your husband. But Argus was trying to kill me. And so, too, with the others. I was defending myself, and I believe that man, or woman, has the right to defend himself or herself. With deadly force, if necessary."

"Then, there's your answer, John. You have a right to seek vengeance for your men. Fergus would kill you if he got the chance."

"You don't know that. He was after you, Emma, not me, when he murdered my men."

She shook her head, threw up her hands in confusion.

"Then don't kill him. I don't care. I just want Eva back."

"If I don't have to kill him, I won't."

"Fine. But I'll tell you something about Fergus. If you think he would ever forget you interfered with his life and his plans, you would be sadly mistaken. If you don't kill him, he will come after you again and again. I saw a dog bark at him when he was about fourteen. The dog ran away, but Fergus followed him and cut the dog's head clean off. And he never batted an eye."

"There are men like that."

"He was just a boy then. That just isn't normal, John."

"No. It's extreme, I admit."

"Well, you worry over whether or not you're doing right when it comes to Fergus. But if he has so much as harmed a hair on her head, I'll shoot him myself."

"You surprise me, Emma."

She laughed in an almost hysterical fashion. "Then you don't know what a mother is," she said.

He stood up. He ejected the spent cartridge in his cylinder and pulled another round from his belt and pushed it into the empty chamber, then slid his pistol back in its holster.

"Be slow going in the dark," he told her. He stretched his hand out to her, and she took it and rose from her bedroll to stand close to him.

"At least we'll be getting closer to Denver with each step."

"Yes. We can see the road by starlight."

"John, I'm glad you're with me."

She leaned even closer.

"I am, too, Emma."

She opened her mouth as if to say something, but instead, she drew in a breath and turned away. She stooped down to pick up her bedding. He wanted to grab her and kiss her at that moment, but he knew that this was not the time. She was vulnerable and weak. The snakebite and her daughter's predicament put her in a hard, lonely place. He was not going to take advantage of the circumstances. If there was to be something more between them, then that time would come soon enough.

But he was wrestling with his own emotions, his feelings for her. He was questioning whether or not he was just as vulnerable as she. They were alone, it was night, and she smelled like mountain flowers.

"Need any help?" he asked as he walked to his own bedroll.

"No," she said. "I'm fine. Just that little stitch in my leg."

"If you feel light-headed or dizzy, you let me know, hear?"

"I will," she said.

They were on the road several minutes later. Side by side, they rode, so close they could have touched each other. He kept looking at her face with sidelong glances, not just to see if she was all right, but because she looked so beautiful in the evening light. She had helped him kick sand on the fire and, even in that dimness afterward, he could see her face and feel her closeness, smell the musk of her, and he wanted her then more than he had when the fire was bright in her eyes and illuminating her face.

They rode in silence, but it was as if each could sense the other's thoughts. When he looked at her, he saw that she was looking at him. She smiled at him and he smiled back.

In that wordless exchange, he felt a bond between them. It made his chest swell and gave him a feeling of manliness.

As for Emma, she was grateful that John was riding

alongside her and that they had this time together. She felt more like a woman than she ever had before. It was as if a contentment were building inside her, despite her worries and her fears. It was a strange feeling for her, because it was completely new and as surprising as a sudden sunrise blossoming in the window of a dark and lonely room.

15

AFTER BEN READ THE NOTE ON EMMA'S DOOR, HE FELT THE pressure of time and distance. There was no telling how long John and Emma had been gone, but he could figure his own time in taking the wagon back to the ranch, saddling up Thunder and seeing to his grub, grain for the horse, and filling four canteens. Then, there had been the slow ride to Butterfly Creek.

How long had Emma and John stayed in town? Long enough for her to saddle up her horse and pack supplies for the ride to Denver. He rode away from town and took the shortest route to the Pueblo-Denver road. He glanced up at the sun and estimated that it was past noon. He had plenty of daylight left to catch up to John and Emma.

He rode down a game trail that he and John had ridden many times before. It was little used now since settlers had come to Butterfly Creek. The deer gave the town a wide berth and sought water in other places along the creek. But the trail brought back memories as he noticed how nature was starting to take it back, erase the old hoof marks, and grow grass where the earth had been worn bare.

He hit the Denver road as a flapping crow fought off a half dozen magpies ragging it with squawking invective, their black-and-white plumage in stark contrast to the crow's velvety, blue black feathers. The noisy birds disappeared into the trees and the road took on a hush that amplified its emptiness. The buttes and mesas glistened reddish gold in the sunlight and looked like ancient citadels or fortresses blasted by wind and snow and rain over the centuries. It was a desolate landscape but hauntingly beautiful under the radiance of the afternoon sun. Ben put Thunder into an easy gallop while the horse was still relatively fresh.

To his left, the shining mountains glistened with light, the snowcapped peaks marking the range that stretched from Mexico to Canada, massive and majestic, with a muscular grade that never failed to stir something deep in Ben, something close to awe and a reverence that was beyond explanation.

He let Thunder walk for another mile or two, then ticked his flanks with his blunt spurs, watching his hide for signs of sweat or foam, listening to his breathing. It was hot, and the horse could founder easily if his lungs tired and he sweated too much. He batted away flies that chased him across the prairie and slapped a couple on Thunder's neck and hips.

Ben thought about the two dead men and how they had died. He tried to picture the kind of man who would sneak up on another and slit his throat. There was something heartless and brutal about that method of killing. And, he thought, perhaps something cowardly about a man so secretive and skulking. Such a man would have little regard for human life. And to slit a man's throat, cutting off his air, the very source of life, was unspeakably vicious.

Yet, such a man had killed two good hands, Juanito and Carlos. Without warning and for no good reason except to send a message to John Savage. The man was connected to Emma in some way, that he knew. Did she know him? How did he know her? Was he someone from her past, a secret lover she had rejected? He didn't know, but he thought of gentle Emma and a man who would kill to gain her favor.

Ben would like to fry the sonofabitch in oil.

That thought should have satisfied him. But he knew it was only wishful thinking, and he could not get the images of those cut throats out of his mind. He could picture the faceless man coming up behind Juanito and grabbing him. Then, he surmised, the man would have pulled Juanito's head back and slashed his throat. So close, so personal. The thought gave Ben the shudders.

And what of Juanito's last seconds of life? He could not have known that his life would be cut so short, nor even that his throat would open up and his blood spill out even as he gasped his last bloody breath. That last moment, when blood was pouring from his wound. Then Juanito would have known that his life was flowing away. He probably looked into eternity at that moment. Then, Ben thought, all memory of his life would have vanished in a twinkling.

He shook his head to shake out the bloody thoughts.

The sun inched across the blue arc of the sky and Ben tilted his hat so that the brim shaded the left side of his face.

Ahead of him, sheep crossed the road, heading toward the mountains. A small black-and-white dog kept them bunched up and moving. Behind the sheep, a sombreroed shepherd with a crook ambled in their wake, a skeletal man wearing shabby white trousers and a grimy gray shirt. Ben raised a hand and wiggled it, but the shepherd only nodded as he crossed the road. Hundreds of sheep streamed to the foothills and looked like scattered clumps of cauliflowers.

"Goin' to the high country for the summer, Thunder," Ben said to his horse. "Wisht I was goin' with 'em."

Ben rode on, into the soft dusk that erased the splendor of the setting sun, and the breeze turned chill. He reached back and pulled his jacket off the top of his bedroll and slipped it on. Later, just before dark, he stopped and gave Thunder a couple of handfuls of grain and poured water into his hat so that the horse could drink.

"Not too much, old boy," he said. "We got a long ways to go. This is to put some steam in your brisket."

The road was empty, lonesome. Ben hummed to himself and tried whistling a tune, but his heart wasn't in it. Besides, he liked the silence better than his whistling. He kept Thunder at a steady pace, varying his speed. He had no idea whether or not he had gained any ground on John and Emma. The road was a mesmerizing scrawl dusted by starlight and when the moon came up, it turned to a dull pewter, stretching into the blackness beyond.

He had lost all track of time but knew that he had only been riding a couple of hours when he saw something ahead of him. His heart jumped in his chest, but he instinctively dropped his right hand to the butt of his pistol. He saw the dark blobs, but they grew no closer. He put Thunder into a trot and watched as the dark shapes grew larger.

Then they disappeared, and he slowed Thunder.

Perhaps, he thought, he had seen a couple of stray cows, or elk, that had wandered down out of the mountains.

He reached that point in the road where he had last seen the apparitions and reined Thunder to a halt.

"Anybody there?" he said into the darkness around him.

There was only a silence that seemed to grow more ominous by the second.

"Ho there. Be you man or beast?"

Another silence, and Ben turned Thunder in a circle to look back down the road and to either side.

"Ben," came a voice that he recognized as John's.

A moment later, two riders emerged from the side of the road and approached him.

"John, you can scare a man half to death," Ben said.

"We thought you were a brigand, Ben."

Emma laughed, and the two came into full view.

"A brigand? What the hell's a brigand?"

"A highwayman. A robber. Your horse worn out?"

"Nope. Where in hell are we?"

"We passed Castle Rock an hour ago. I can see the lights of Denver if I look hard enough."

"You all right, Miss Emma?"

"Fairly tolerable, Ben," she said. "I'm glad you caught up with us."

"Now that you're here, Ben, let's all get some shut-eye," John said.

"I could use the rest," Ben said. "So could Thunder."

They rode out onto the prairie and found a spot beneath a massive rock outcropping that resembled an old castle worn down by wind and rain.

They slept late the next day, much to Emma's discomfort. They lost more time when her horse got a rock in its shoe. It took Ben the better part of an hour to remove it and hammer the nail back in.

The three rode all the next day and into the night.

"We should be in Denver before midnight," John said when it turned dark.

"Then what?"

"We go to the Larimer and get Eva," John said.

"Then, let's get to it," Ben said.

The three of them rode into Denver and galloped along

Sixteenth Street, turned onto Larimer, and started looking for the hotel. Streetlamps glowed and many of the saloons were open, their yellow lights spilling onto the street, the sounds of clinking glasses, melodic guitars, and raking fiddles underlining the sound of loud voices and bad singing.

They saw the lights and the shadowy sign of the Larimer Hotel. Out front, four men and a young girl mounted horses.

"Into the shadows," John whispered to Ben and Emma. He turned Gent to the opposite side of the street and pulled on the bit to stop him. Emma and Ben sidled up next to him.

"What is it?" Emma asked.

"Shhh. Just watch," John said, pointing down the street. "Don't say anything until they pass."

John heard her gasp as the horses turned away from the hotel and headed their way.

Thunder whickered and Ben jerked on the reins to quiet him.

The riders came close but did not look their way. Emma rose up in her stirrups and craned her neck.

John swung his arm and put the flat of his hand over her mouth.

Emma's eyes widened and she dropped back into the saddle.

She looked over at John. He shook his head as the riders passed without seeing them.

When they disappeared down the street, John drew back· his hand.

"That was Eva with those men," she whispered. "And that man in front was Fergus."

"I know," John said.

"You let them get away." He could feel the heat of her anger.

"They're going somewhere," John said. "We'll follow them."

"But what about Eva?"

"We'll get her back when the time comes."

"We missed an opportunity, John. They were so close."

"Patience, Emma. That wasn't the time. Eva was in the middle of that bunch and if we'd opened fire on them, she would have been the first to die."

"I agree," Ben said, although he wasn't asked.

"There'll be few riders out tonight. We'll follow them. They may be leaving town or they might be up to something."

"I don't care," Emma said. "I want my daughter back."

"It must be almost midnight, Emma. Fergus is going somewhere and he's taking Eva with him. There must be a reason since he's supposed to be waiting for you."

Emma breathed through her nose but said nothing.

"Let's go," John said. "Easy does it. We don't want them to know that we're following them."

"What if they're taking Eva somewhere to murder her?" Emma asked.

"Fergus doesn't need three other men with him to do that."

They rode back down the street. In a few minutes they saw the riders far ahead of them. They didn't seem to be in any hurry. John, Emma, and Ben followed at a safe distance, neither they nor their horses making enough sound to carry to the ears of the riders they were following.

They drifted down a street that led to the east. Then, there were no more streetlamps and no more buildings. But the moon was high and the riders barely visible in the distance where only trees grew and a well-rutted road speared into the night like a softly glazed ribbon that was white as bone.

16

FERGUS AND THE OTHERS LEFT THE ROAD WHEN THEY GOT INTO
the rolling land called Cherry Hills. When he spotted the
first house, a white frame structure atop a small knoll,
he called a halt.

"You boys know what to do," he said. "Jubal, you ride up
to Bobbitt's lane and watch the front. Fred, you and Dick
go around to the back and wait. Look for any lamps inside
and be real quiet."

"Where will you and the gal be?" Jubal asked.

"We'll go in the front. Dick, you and Fred will go in the
back and let me and the gal in through the front door. Remember. No noise. No shooting. Neighbors might hear us."

"Right, Boss," Dick said.

"You stay right close, gal," Fergus said.

"Where would I go?" she said, her voice quavering with
terror.

"No place."

"I don't even know where we are."

"You just stay close if you want to see another sunrise."

Eva kept her thoughts to herself. She feared Fergus, and she was lost in all the trees and the gentle rolling hills.

The Bobbitt house was in the center of a semicircle of homes atop a hill. The other houses were spaced less than an acre apart. All but one, including Bobbitt's, were dark. One house had a lamp burning in an upstairs window. It glowed a pale yellow in the darkness. Fergus looked at it, but saw no movement behind the thin shade.

Fergus gestured for Dick and Fred to dismount and break into the Bobbitt house through the back door.

He watched as Fred approached the back door on foot. He saw Fred turn the knob. To his surprise, the door opened. He and Dick disappeared inside.

Then he and Eva rode around to the front. By the time they got there, the front door was open. Jubal was dismounting. He entered the house first. Moments later, Eva and Fergus walked inside and down the hallway.

The four men and Eva stood at the foot of the stairs, listening.

The boards in the house ticked in the silence.

Fergus beckoned to the others, who followed him into the living room. There, he lit a lamp. He handed it to Jubal. He found another, struck a match, and watched the wick flare with flame. He handed that one to Fred.

They all followed him down the hall to one of the bedrooms. The door was closed but unlocked. He turned the knob very slowly and pushed the door open. He pushed Eva ahead of him and entered the room. He motioned for Jubal to follow him.

There was a man asleep on the bed. A young man. Jubal shone the lamp on him. He held it high enough so that Fergus could see Jubal's face. He mouthed the name silently: "Jerome."

Fergus nodded.

He drew his bowie knife, shoved Eva into Jubal, and stepped close to the bed.

He placed his left hand over Jerry Bobbitt's mouth and tilted his head back so that the man's Adam's apple jutted from his neck. He quickly sliced through the neck, cutting deep into the flesh. Blood bubbled out of the wound. Jerome gurgled as his eyes flew open in surprise. Then, both eyes clouded over and closed as the young man's body jerked spasmodically for a few seconds and then was still.

Eva opened her mouth and a tiny squeak escaped her lips. Jubal clamped a hand over her mouth.

"You scream, Eva," Fergus whispered to her, "and I'll slit your throat, hear?"

She nodded and Jubal took his hand away. The three tiptoed out of the room. Dick and Fred were waiting on the other side of another bedroom door. Fergus turned the knob and the door opened. He and Fred entered Phillip Bobbitt's bedroom. He was asleep, lying on his stomach. His face was turned toward the wall, and he was snoring gently, deep in slumber.

Fergus grabbed a clump of hair on the back of Phil's head. He put the knife to his throat so fast the man had no time to cry out. Fergus cut deep into Phil's throat, slicing it from ear to ear. Air and blood gushed from the man's throat as his eyes opened wide in shock and surprise. Eva shuddered and covered her face with both hands. Fergus stepped away and wiped the bloody blade on his trousers.

"Upstairs," he said to Jubal as he headed for the open door.

Dick led the way up the stairs. He and Fred had been in the house before, when the Bobbitts were at work. They knew where each person slept and they knew where Earl Bobbitt kept his safe.

The lamps cast an eerie light on the walls. Shadows danced like dark wraiths on the floor and ceiling. Dick opened the door to the master bedroom. They all rushed in on tiptoe. The lamp illuminated the bed where Earl and Anella were fast asleep. Fred took a lamp and walked to the tall wardrobe and stood beside it. Jubal grabbed Anella and clamped a hand over her mouth. She made muffled sounds as he pulled her from under the covers. She kicked and struggled to no avail.

Fergus smacked Earl across the face to wake him up. He put the blade of his knife a few inches from Earl's face.

"Don't make a sound, Bobbitt," Fergus growled, his voice low in his throat.

"Wha?" Earl Bobbitt said.

"Get up and open that safe or your woman's dead meat."

Bobbitt's eyes widened as he saw the men in the room. The big one was holding Anella. Her eyes were wide in terror, a hand across her mouth.

Bobbitt threw off the covers and stepped onto the floor.

"Don't hurt her," he said. He wore a long white night-shirt. Anella was wearing a pink gown that appeared to have been made out of silk. She no longer struggled in Jubal's grip, but stood there, her eyes wide with terror.

Fred opened the doors of the wardrobe. The black hulk of the safe gleamed in the lamplight. Gold paint on the fili-greed borders glistened, and the silver of the combination lock and the leaden four-spoked wheel above it shone amid wavering shadows.

"Damn you," Bobbitt said as Fergus pushed him toward the safe.

"Shut up and open it," Fergus said.

Bobbitt leaned down and moved the numbers around to the left. He stopped on seventeen and then spun the wheel to the right, stopping at the number four. He rolled to three more numbers, and they all heard a slight tick in the safe's mechanism. Bobbitt reached for the spokes, but Fergus grabbed him by the nape of his gown and pulled him backward.

"Open it, Fred," Fergus said.

Fred spun the wheel and pulled on it. The door swung open. There were stacks of money on the floor, all neatly bundled and tied. Fred opened drawers and revealed more currency.

"Dick, get them pillowcases," Fergus ordered.

Dick walked to the bed and stripped the pillows, tossing them on the floor. He returned with four of them, then he and Fred began pulling money from the safe and filling up the pillowcases.

"You get it all?" Fergus asked Fred.

"Yep. They's some jewelry in one of the drawers."

"Throw those in, too," Fergus said.

Fred pulled out a drawer and emptied it into a bag Dick held open. The jewelry slid from the drawer and tinkled into the makeshift sack.

"You got what you came for," Bobbitt said. "Now get out."

Fergus looked at him in disgust, his mouth curved in a sneer.

He walked over to Anella and pulled Jubal's hand away from her mouth.

Jubal released her and stepped back.

"No," she said, as Fergus stepped in close. He swiped the knife across her throat as Bobbitt watched in horror. Blood dripped from the wide smile Fergus had carved into her throat and she crumpled to the floor.

Bobbitt rushed toward Fergus.

He walked into the point of Fergus's knife square at the center of his throat. He started to swing a fist at Fergus, but

Fergus shoved the knife deep, twisted it, and tore half of Bobbitt's throat.

Bobbitt gurgled as blood spurted from his wound. Fergus sidestepped and withdrew his knife. He grabbed Bobbitt's arm, twisted it behind his back. Bobbitt fell to his knees. Fergus slashed the other side of Bobbitt's throat and the dead man pitched forward. He hit the floor with a resounding thump, his hands quivering. He gave two kicks with one leg and then lay still.

Fergus wiped his blade on his trouser leg.

Eva stood there, both eyes squinched like tiny fists.

Dick and Fred hefted two sacks each, slinging them over their shoulders.

"Let's hit the trail," Fergus said as he slid his knife back in its sheath.

They all walked back down the stairs.

"Fill all the saddlebags," Fergus told Fred and Dick. "Don't let none of the money show."

"What you figure we got, Fergus?" Dick asked.

"Maybe ten years' wages for each of us, with a big bonus left over."

Outside, they all gathered together as Dick and Fred divided up the money, stuffing all the saddlebags with the bills, leaving some in the pillowcases. They filled Eva's saddlebags as well.

Then they all rode away from the Bobbitt house. None of them noticed the man in the window. He had turned off his lamp and stood there, watching as the money was transferred and the robbers left. He waited a long time before he dressed, strapped on his pistol, and walked downstairs. He took a rifle from his gun case and waited a while longer at the front door.

He trembled, afraid of what he might find when he

walked over to Bobbitt's house. He opened the door and saw lights flickering in the downstairs windows.

He had the eerie feeling that ghosts were wandering through the Bobbitt house. The windows flickered with light and shadows as if nobody was at home and they had left the lamps burning for their return.

17

---◆---

LEAF SHADOWS FROM OAKS AND MAPLES DAPPLED THE ROAD. THE moon created stone pools in the ruts and hoof marks. Somewhere an owl hooted, sounding like a barnyard rooster with laryngitis in the still night. John's senses sharpened as he stared down the road with the strong feeling that something had changed.

He felt that the silence had suddenly deepened, that something was missing. He no longer saw riders ahead of them, yet the road was fairly straight through the stands of trees that bordered both sides of the road. The silence seemed to shriek at him, tear at his ears with rabid claws that demanded he hear hoofbeats, a cough, a snort, a horse's soft whicker, some small sound that indicated life in a desolate landscape of shadows and pale light that was like soundless marble.

"I don't see 'em no more," Ben whispered as he leaned close to John's ear.

"We must have fallen too far behind," John whispered back.

"They're gone," Emma said, her whisper the loudest of all.

"They outfoxed us," Ben said.

"You two wait here," John said. "I'll see if I can figure this out."

"Be careful, John," Emma said as he rode off into the darkness.

A hundred yards away, John dismounted so that he would be closer to the ground and could, perhaps, make out the tracks of the riders they had been following. He saw the hoof marks, five sets of tracks heading in the same direction. He followed these and saw where they had all stopped. He walked a few paces beyond and saw no more tracks. So, he thought, they had split up. He walked back to where the tracks were all stationary and started walking a small circle.

He isolated the track that he recognized as belonging to the horse being ridden by Fergus. His horse, and another, veered off into the grass. The blades were just beginning to spring back, but he could make them out by stooping over. His eyes burned under the strain. He walked through inky trees and their deep shadows. He took out his knife and cut a blaze on one of the oaks. Then he mounted Gent and rode back to get Emma and Ben.

"Find anything?" Ben asked.

"They split up. But I think I can track Fergus. And I think Eva may be riding alongside him."

"Oh, I hope so," Emma breathed.

"Follow me. When I start tracking again, you'll have to follow. And look out for an ambush."

"Lead the way," Ben said.

John found the blaze he had made. He dismounted, handed the reins of his horse to Ben.

He began tracking. It was hard, slow work. The tracks angled off from the others in a straight line, then turned right. It was like walking in tar. Only the grasses yielded up their secrets, but it took all of his concentration to see where the blades had been crushed.

It was slow going, and John knew they were losing valuable time. He wondered where all the riders were going and why they had separated. The mystery deepened since the tracks foretold no destination.

John lost sight of the tracks and had to backtrack and search for them. The trees grew thick in that section, and he saw no signs of habitation. Then they heard the muffled sounds of many hoofbeats.

They were very loud at first, then faded away, just as John emerged from a grove of oak trees and saw lights burning in two houses. He saw the dim figure of a man walking between the two houses.

"Reckon that was them, John?" Ben said.

John grabbed the reins from Ben and climbed into the saddle.

"It damn sure wasn't the cavalry."

"Oh, John, they're probably getting away," Emma said.

"Likely," John said and spurred Gent into a gallop. He headed toward the walking man. As he drew closer, he saw that the man had a rifle slung atop one shoulder. As John, Emma, and Ben approached, he jerked the rifle off his shoulder and swung it toward them.

"You all just stop right there," the man shouted.

John reined to a halt. Emma and Ben pulled up next to him.

"We're following four men and a girl," John said. "We mean you no harm."

"They run off from Bobbitt's a while ago. You with 'em?"

"No, the girl has been kidnapped by those men. She's the daughter of the woman riding with me."

"Come up close real slow so's I can see your faces," the man said.

"You mind pointing that rifle somewhere else?" Ben called out.

The man swung the rifle slightly away from them, but still held it to his shoulder.

John and the others rode up until the man ordered them to halt once again.

"I'm Emma Blanchett," she said. "Those men who rode away are murderers and they kidnapped my daughter, Eva."

"That ain't all they done," the man said.

"I'm John Savage and this is my friend, Ben Russell. Mind telling me who you are and what you're talking about?"

"My name is Daniel Chase. I live in that house yonder. I just come from Bobbitt's. I heard a commotion and saw them men and that girl ride off like a bunch of scared rabbits. I knowed they was up to no good."

John rode in close, and Chase lowered his rifle.

"Who are the Bobbitts?" he asked.

"Bobbitt Freight. Front door was open, so I walked in and called out Earl's and Anella's names. Didn't get no answer, so I walked down the hall to Jerry's room. Godamighty, he was dead, his throat cut open like a watermelon. I figure they're all dead, but I got real sick when I saw Jerry and hightailed it out of there. I figure the whole family's dead. Murdered in their sleep."

"Any idea why they were murdered?" John asked.

"Earl kept a lot of money in his safe. Didn't trust the banks. Robbery, maybe. I don't know."

"Is that the house?" John asked, pointing to the one off to his left.

Chase nodded.

"Where are you going now?" John asked.

"I was going to ride into Denver and get a constable out here."

"You do that. We're going to see if anybody's still alive in there."

"I'll bet they're all dead," Chase said.

"Go get the constable. Can you tell me which way they rode when they left?"

Chase pointed.

"They were headed back to Denver, likely," he said. "They was all in a powerful hurry."

They left Chase as he walked back to his house and rode up to Bobbitt's. They tied their reins to the hitchrail and walked up to the house. The front door was still open and they all went inside. Emma was trembling. John's right hand closed around the grip of his pistol.

"That must be the hallway Chase went down," Ben said.

"Ben, you and Emma wait here. And be ready to draw your pistols if any of Fergus's men come back."

John walked down the hallway, his hand still on the Colt's grip. It was dark in the first room he entered, but there was a spray of star and moonlight glimmering through the window. He saw the form of the man on the bed. He smelled the blood and the taint of offal from the relaxed sphincter. He leaned over and saw the young man's slashed throat. He had seen that trademark of Fergus's before, and he recoiled from the ghastly sight.

He tiptoed out of the room and walked down the hall to the other bedroom, his boots making little sound on the rug. There was enough light so that he could see that the other man was dead, too, a hideous scarlet grin gaping on his throat.

"Killed while they slept," he said to Emma and Ben when he returned.

"How many?" Ben asked.

"Two young men." John looked at Emma. Her face was bone white and her blue eyes crinkled in the lamplight.

"Must be Bobbitt's sons," Ben said. "Now what?"

"I'm going to take one of those lamps and go upstairs."

"John, I don't want to stay down here," Emma said.

"You might not like what you see, Emma."

"I don't want to see them. I just want to be close to you."

"I don't fancy stayin' down here by myself," Ben said.

"Grab that other lamp and follow me up, then," John said.

The three climbed the stairs. Ben and John held the oil lamps. The yellow light made the shadows waver and dance. They all entered the Bobbitt bedroom.

"You'd better stay here by the door, Emma," John said.

"I see the safe," she said.

Then she saw the two bodies on the floor and recoiled in horror.

The safe door gaped like some monstrous maw. John stepped over Bobbitt's body and held the lamp so that it shone on the empty shelves.

"Looks like they cleaned Bobbitt out," John said. He stooped over both bodies and saw that their throats were cut.

Ben stood there, gawking at the bodies as if they held some hypnotic quality that turned him mute. His mouth opened, but no sound issued forth. His face wrinkled up in a sour grimace.

"Let's get out of here," John said, his voice pitched low. He put an arm around Emma, who had turned her back on the grisly scene.

He and Emma stepped out of the room. Ben lurched behind them, shaking his head in disbelief.

Downstairs, John put both lamps on a table and left them burning.

"It's going to be hard to track them in the dark," he said. "And, it would take more time than we have."

"We can't just let Fergus get away," Emma said.

"No. We'll ride straight to the Larimer Hotel, see if he's there."

"John, we're buckin' up against four men. And don't forget about Eva."

"I'm not."

"Why, hell, maybe we ought to round up a constable or two afore we just go bargin' in."

"I don't think Fergus will be at the hotel," John said.

"What?" Emma exclaimed.

"I think he and his men, along with Eva, are long gone. But he might have left word where he wants you to meet him, Emma."

"You think so?" she said.

"I'd almost bet on it."

They mounted up and rode down the lane and found the road to Denver.

The truth was, he would not bet on anything at this point. But he knew Fergus wanted Emma, and Eva was his stack of chips in this deadly game. As they rode, he could not get the stench of death out of his nostrils. It seemed to become part of the night itself. He could no longer smell the scent of grasses and trees. There was only the rank odor of death floating on the night air.

18

FERGUS, EVA, AND THE OTHERS RODE INTO LONGMONT, NORTH OF Denver, just as dawn was breaking. In the west, the sky was made of iron. In the east, there was a line of cream across the horizon, with gray streamers of clouds floating in long parallel lines, fluffy loaves of unbaked dough.

Eva slumped in the saddle, half asleep. She was exhausted from the ride, from the mental images that were all shaped like the bellies of butchered hogs. She knew what Fergus had done to those people. She knew he had cut their throats without mercy, without a single pang of conscience. The horror of it would not go away. She had seen hogs butchered, their dead bodies hanging from tree limbs, but what he had done to the Bobbitts was more than she could comprehend.

"We'll put up at the Platte," Fergus told Dick and Fred.

"Best hotel in town," Dick said.

"Best grub in town, too," Fred said.

"Speakin' of grub . . ." Jubal chimed in. He rubbed his empty belly and grinned.

"You could go a week without food," Fergus said.

"Yeah, he could hibernate just like a grizzly bear," Dick said.

"Jubal can go eat while we count the money," Fred said.

"You just shut up about the money, Fred," Fergus said.

"Hell, it's already burnin' holes in my pocket, Fergus." Fred tried a grin on Fergus. It didn't work. Fergus frowned.

"The minute we flash them greenbacks, folks are goin' to get suspicious," Fergus said. "For now, just pretend we're all broke."

"Good idea," Dick said. "Longmont's full of criminals, robbers and such."

The men all laughed as they rode up to the two-story, nondescript Platte Hotel, two blocks off of Main, with lamps glowing in the lobby and an adjoining eatery where a shadowy waiter was spreading light brown cloths on tables.

"We hitchin' up here?" Dick asked.

"Until we get them saddlebags up to my room," Fergus said. "Then you and Jubal can put 'em up at the livery. But don't unsaddle 'em. Just see that they all get grain and water."

"We goin' somewheres else right soon?" Jubal asked.

"Depends on Emma," Fergus said.

"I can't wait to see this gal you're so fixed on," Dick said. "She must be some gal."

"Dick," Fergus said, "you think too damned much."

"I'd just like to know what you got on your mind, Fergus. You don't say much, but I know you got big plans."

"Fred knows some of what I got planned," Fergus said. "And maybe Jubal."

"How come I don't?" Dick said.

"You will, Dick. Pretty damned soon."

Fergus had known these men in prison. During that time,

they had talked, mostly about Colorado, Wyoming, and Utah. Fred and Dick had traveled all over the territory and Jubal had been jailed in Santa Fe for petty theft, had traveled north, all the way to Cheyenne where he had been arrested. All three men had wound up in Texas.

Fergus considered it Fate that had drawn them all together in Huntsville. There was no other explanation. Fergus could think of nothing else but his brother and Emma, little Eva, all settled in Colorado. And by questioning each of the men, he formulated his plans to seek his fortune in the territories with the three of them. Each had known only the criminal life, and he knew how to use them to his advantage. He had big dreams. He considered them useful pawns that he could exploit to fulfill those dreams.

They all entered the Platte Hotel lugging their saddlebags and rifles over their shoulders.

A sleepy desk clerk emerged from a small office and lifted the registration book to the top of the counter.

"Mornin', gents," he said. "Rooms for each of you?"

He was a man in his late forties, with a leaden moustache that drooped his mouth like a horseshoe. He wore a high collar and a cotton string tie dyed black. His eyes were close-set and deep sunk, a pair of shriveled raisins in puckered sockets.

"Four rooms," Fergus said, "all next to each other."

"I believe we can accommodate you, sir. A room for you and your daughter, and three others. That right?"

"Yes," Fergus said. He put a hand on Eva's shoulder to underline the point about her being his daughter.

"That will be two dollars each per night," the clerk said. "No charge for the child."

"One dollar," Fergus said.

The clerk cleared his throat and looked into the eyes of the man who had just diminished the nightly rate.

"Fifty cents for the girl, sir. Each of you must sign the register. Or make your marks."

"We can write our names," Dick said.

"Yes, sir. I believe you have stayed with us before. A few weeks ago, I believe."

"You got a good memory."

"I'm Charles Sweeney," the clerk said. "I never forget a guest's face."

"That could get you in trouble," Fred said, inching forward to sign the register.

"I also know how to keep my mouth shut, sir," Sweeney said. "When it comes to the guests who stay here, my lips are sealed tighter than Granny's Mason jars."

The men all laughed. Eva's head was drooping. It bobbed up, then dropped again.

Sweeney turned to the sidewall and plucked four skeleton keys from the dowels. Each had a room number written on a wooden tag. He dropped them on the counter. They clattered like a clump of costume jewelry. He spread them out.

"All rooms are pretty much the same," Sweeney said as Fred signed the register with a false name, Tom Becker. Fergus put four dollars and a fifty-cent piece in front of Sweeney.

"Just the one night, then?"

"We'll let you know if we're stayin' more'n a day," Fergus said.

The clerk put the money in a cash drawer and wrote out a receipt to a William Smith, the name Fergus used to sign the register.

"We aim to break our fast soon as the dining hall opens," Fergus said.

"Ah, we open for breakfast in about a half hour, Mr. Smith."

"Jubal, you meet us in there, and we'll all grab some grub."

Jubal handed his saddlebags to Dick but kept his rifle. He took his key and went back outside to lead the horses to the livery stable. Fergus and the others clumped up the stairs, keys in hand.

Fergus took the room nearest the stairs. He put his key in the door.

"Bring them saddlebags in my room," he told Dick and Fred. "One of you will have to wait on breakfast. The least hungriest."

"I'll watch over the, ah, the saddlebags," Fred said.

"And that don't mean countin' or filchin' any of it," Fergus said as the lock clicked and the door opened.

Eva stumbled into the room, half asleep. Her feet felt like her shoes were sash weights and her back ached as if someone had set fire to it.

"I just want to go to bed," she said, stumbling toward the comforter-covered blanket atop the mattress in a wrought-iron frame.

Fergus grabbed her hand and pulled her back.

"You're gonna eat first, little gal, or you won't be nothin' but a shadder come noon."

The saddlebags landed on the center of the bed to a creaking of slats and springs as the men tossed them in a leathery heap.

Fergus poured water into the tin basin atop the chest of drawers and splashed his face. Dick walked to the window and looked out at the gray morning, the mountain range in the distance where Longs Peak stood higher than the others, its crown garbed in soft ermine. Fred sat in the easy chair and watched Eva collapse at the foot of the bed, looking like a large limp doll. He stretched out his legs and moved his toes inside his boots, wriggling them until he felt the blood restore them to life.

Fergus wiped his face dry with a fresh hand towel. Dick turned away from the window.

"Looks like rain, Fergus," he said.

"Maybe in the mountains," Fergus said. "Not here."

"I'll bet it hits us," Dick said.

"Don't matter none. We ain't goin' nowheres today."

"Good. I'm plumb wore down to a nubbin."

"I can't wait to see how much we got from Bobbitt," Fred said.

Fergus fixed him with a look as sharp as a barbed spear.

"You know, Fred," Fergus said, "you ought to think more about what that clerk Sweeney said a while ago."

"What's that, Fergus?"

"About keepin' your mouth shut tight as a Mason jar."

"Oh, yeah. Granny's Mason jar," Fred said, stifling a yawn with the back of his hand. "Hell, ain't nobody but us here."

"It's a bad habit, Fred. You might spill the beans in a place full of ears."

"Not me."

"Just don't talk about nothin' we done or what we're gonna do. You got that?"

"Hell, I don't know what we're gonna do, Fergus. You don't tell us nothin'."

"And that's the way it's gonna be," Fergus said. He walked to the bed and shook Eva awake.

"Come on," he said. "Time to eat."

She turned over and blinked her eyes.

"Up," he said.

"I'm hungry as a bear," Dick said, walking toward the door.

"Eat fast," Fred said. "My belly's touchin' my backbone."

Fergus ushered Eva out of the room and into the hallway where Dick was waiting.

He stuck his head back into the room.

"You keep an eye on things, Fred." Fergus locked the door.

"If he touches any of that money," Fergus muttered, "he'll be a dead prisoner."

Fergus started for the stairs, pulling Eva with him by the hand.

In the distant mountains, behind Longs Peak, there was a faint rumble of thunder. Outside, the street was painted a soft gray and the town still slumbered under a sky filling with long elephantine clouds.

19

DAN CHASE DIDN'T GET VERY FAR. HIS GALLOP INTO DENVER WAS cut short when his horse, a slender, sure-footed Missouri trotter, stepped into a gopher hole. His right foreleg snapped at the ankle. The horse shrieked in pain and Chase flew out of the saddle as his horse collapsed beneath him.

The horse rolled in agony. Dan kicked out of the stirrups as the horse fell to one side, thrashing in pain. Dan landed hard on his chest. He felt the air whoosh out of his lungs in a single gust. The dark earth spun in a crazy spiral for a second as if the trees were flying up to the sky and the stars were tumbling downward in a blur of jiggling lights that entered his brain and mingled with the dancing stars that were already there. His head struck something hard, like a rock, as his neck snapped backward, then forward as if his neck were made of rubber. The lights dimmed, the stars vanished, and then there was only a peaceful blackness as he lost consciousness.

A tiny trickle of blood seeped from his hairline and

streamed down through his sideburn and onto his cheek. Air trickled back into his lungs as he lay there, sprawled like a scarecrow blown down by a strong wind.

John heard the horse's squealing whinny that soared to the high register of the musical scale. Emma and Ben heard it, too, and stiffened in their saddles. There was something almost humanlike in the ear-piercing scream and she thought of Eva. Ben knew that it was a horse, either badly hurt or badly frightened.

"You two wait here," John said. "It's right up ahead. I'll see what it is."

"It's a horse," Ben said.

John ignored him and rode on, his eyes straining to see what might lie ahead. He walked Gent along one edge of the road, ready to kick him in the flanks and run for cover.

He saw movement at ground level. The horse was struggling to free its foot from the gopher hole, kicking at the ground with its hind legs, flailing the air with one foreleg, breathy squeals spurting from its throat, its rubbery nostrils quivering as its head bobbed up and down like an oil pump.

Crickets sawed their dark concertos in the grass. The sizzling of their songs rose and fell in a somber cascade as John dismounted and bent over the unconscious man. He leaned down close to Chase's mouth and felt hot breath blow against his ear. He shook the man's shoulders gently and turned him over.

Dan's downed horse squealed in agony.

"Chase, wake up," John said.

"Uhhn," Dan groaned.

"I'm going to put your horse out of its misery."

Dan's eyes fluttered and he tried to sit up.

"Just lie still until your head clears," John said. He got to his feet, walked over to the stricken animal, and drew his pistol. He put the barrel close to a spot between the horse's

eyes and pulled the trigger. The explosion boomed in the
silence and stilled all the crickets. The horse thrashed one
last time as blood oozed from the hole in its head. Its neck
arched and then relaxed as the last of its breath left its lungs.

Dan got to his feet and staggered over to his horse.

"My God, man, you killed my horse. You killed Willie."

John opened the cylinder gate of his Colt, worked the
plunger, and ejected the empty brass hull of the .45. He slid
a fresh cartridge from his belt into the magazine and closed
the gate, then holstered his pistol.

"Horse's leg was broke," he said.

Tears flooded Dan's cheeks.

"I know, I know," he mumbled and crumpled up in grief.
He dropped to his knees and embraced the horse's neck, his
head against its hide.

John let him cry and walked a few feet away.

"Ben," he called. "Come on."

A few seconds later, Ben and Emma rode up. By then,
Dan was on his feet, swaying drunkenly over the body of
his horse. He reached down and loosened the cinch strap,
pulled the saddle from the horse's back. He took off his
bridle, walked around to the other side, and jerked his rifle
from its scabbard.

He walked over to John, rifle in his hand, bridle slung
over his shoulder.

"Can I hitch a ride into town?" he said.

"Sure," John said. "Climb up behind Ben there. Sorry
about your horse."

"I'd've done the same thing," Dan said. "Thanks for sav-
ing me from that chore."

Ben held out an arm, pulled his boot out of his left stirrup. Dan grabbed his hand and pulled himself up. He swung
a leg over Ben's horse and sat on its rump behind the cantle.

"What—what did you find at Bobbitt's?" Dan asked John as he climbed into the saddle. "Was Earl . . ."

"Four people dead," John said. "Three men and a woman. Did you know them well?"

"Earl was my good friend. Anella, she was a fine woman. And the boys . . ."

He choked up then and couldn't finish. He laid his rifle crossways on his lap and pulled out a kerchief, wiped his eyes, his slobbering mouth.

"You all set, Ben? Let's go," John said. He clucked to Gent and turned him toward Denver.

"John, wait a minute," Emma said.

John pulled on the reins. Gent stopped.

"What is it?"

"There's no need to leave Mr. Chase's saddle here. By morning it will be soaked with dew. Besides, animals could chew on the leather and just ruin it."

"What do you want me to do, drag it?" John said, with more than a trace of sarcasm in his voice.

"I was thinking that you could strap the saddle to my saddle and I could ride double with you, John."

Did he detect an air of superiority in Emma's voice? Perhaps, but she made sense, he decided.

"Now, why didn't I think of that?" John said.

Ben chuckled.

"Because women are more practical than men," Emma said.

Ben snorted. "She's got you there, Johnny," he said.

"I'll get the saddle, Emma. You climb down and we'll ride double into town. On Gent here."

"I'm glad you see it my way," she said, and this time he knew Emma was sticking her barbs into him. He felt like an animal running a gauntlet of dart throwers.

He slid out of his saddle and walked over to where Chase's saddle was pinned under the dead horse. He grabbed it by the horn and jerked it free, lugged it over to Emma's horse, where she stood, holding her reins.

"Any particular way you want me to lash this saddle onto yours?" he asked, with more than a pinch of sarcasm salting his voice.

Starlight freckled her face with silver. He could see her mouth wrinkle in a tired smile like that of a patient person dealing with an imbecilic child.

"Well, if you really want to know, John," she said, "I think if you put Mr. Chase's saddle on my saddle backward, it might be easy to tie down pretty tight so that it won't fall off."

"Let's try it your way," he said, tight-lipped, as if his words were laden with a bitter-tasting poison.

He slung the saddle up atop hers and settled it in the leather cradle.

"Fits like a glove," he said. "Slightly tilted, but she'll ride if I tie her down."

He cut two thongs from Chase's saddle, lengthened his stirrups so that he could pull them beneath the belly of Emma's horse. He tied the stirrups together with the thongs, then rocked the saddle from side to side. It held.

"My," Emma said, "aren't you the adaptable one? I thought you might have to use your rope. Of course you've ruined Mr. Chase's saddle by cutting off those dangling thongs."

"You know, Emma," he said as he gazed down at her mocking eyes, "you can be mighty critical when a man's in a hurry and trying to do his best."

"Oh, I'm not critical at all, John. After all, isn't necessity the mother of invention?"

"I can do without the homilies, too," he said and stomped

toward his horse. He climbed up into the saddle, then reached down for her outstretched hand. He pulled her up after she put a dainty foot in his stirrup. She swung a leg over Gent's rump and snugged up against him. She wrapped her arms around John's waist and gave him a squeeze that forced air out of his lungs.

"You don't need to tie me on, John," she whispered as he tightened the muscles in his diaphragm.

"No, I reckon not," he said and patted the back of one of her hands.

"Mmm," she murmured. "You feel good." She moved her upper torso so that her breasts mashed against his back and rubbed him back and forth.

"You do that any more and I'll have to put you on backward like that saddle," he said.

"Is that a promise or a threat?" she cooed.

John chuckled, then turned to Ben.

"You take the lead, Ben. Chase, you tell him where we can find that constable. I'll lead Emma's horse right behind me."

He turned Gent, rode over to Emma's horse, and grabbed up its reins. Ben rode ahead with his cargo of Dan Chase.

They rode into Denver and pulled up in front of the Constabulary Headquarters on Colfax Avenue. The buildings were dark.

"Nobody here," Ben said.

Chase slid from behind Ben's back and landed on the ground.

"They're all asleep, likely," he said. "I'll roust 'em up."

John and Emma rode up and watched Chase walk to the door of the main building.

Chase began pounding on the door with both fists.

A feeble light illuminated the windows. Someone inside approached the door. The light wobbled in the officer's hand.

"I hope this won't take long," Emma whispered to John. "Are you going to tell them about Eva?"

"I'm just going to tell them what they need to know," he said.

"They'll ask us why we went to that house," she said. "You'll have to tell them."

He patted one of Emma's hands.

"Does lying count as a necessity?" he said. "I might have to invent a good story."

"You catch on quick, John," she said, and gave him a hearty squeeze with both arms. She rubbed her breasts against his back in a playful manner.

"You want to keep riding double, Emma? Or should I cut Chase's saddle loose?"

"Whatever is your pleasure," she said, her voice soft and silky as she stretched her neck and kissed him gently on the back of his neck.

He almost turned around and grappled with her, wanting to taste those lips that had made the hairs on the back of his neck stiffen and rise like electrified wires.

The door opened and a man in a white nightshirt appeared, holding the lamp high so that it shone in Dan's face.

John knew that the long night was going to get even longer. Meanwhile, four men had gotten away with robbery and murder. And one of them was also guilty of kidnapping. By the time the constable got dressed and saddled his horse, those four men might be long gone.

He was already inventing a story that might work so that they would not have to bear witness to the gruesome murders. He slid out of the saddle and untied the thongs binding the stirrups of Chase's saddle to Emma's horse. He pulled it from her saddle and laid it on its side, next to the building's foundation.

Dan looked over at him. He was in the middle of a sentence.

John helped Emma mount her horse, then climbed back into his own saddle.

"Just a minute," the constable said.

"Dan Chase can handle it from here," John said. "He knows more than we do."

The three rode off, down Colfax. They headed for Larimer Street through an empty lightless town, the ghosts of buildings looming on either side, deserted under a black sky full of argentine diamonds that twinkled mindlessly over oceans of space. Somewhere, they heard the faint sound of a guitar and the clacking of Mexican castanets.

20

LONGMONT WAS A YOUNG TOWN, A TOWN STILL GROWING, LIKE some straggly, undernourished weed, yet pulsing with the raw energy of young men determined to saw and nail lumber into prosperous business establishments and comfortable homes. The city was barely six years old and had become an important stage stop, a gathering place for hunters and trappers before they ventured into the vastness of the Rocky Mountains. It boasted a taxidermist, a group of outfitters and guides, a store that sold fishing gear, and a gun shop. The Union Hotel was the nicest in town, but the Platte was preferred by wayfarers, hunting and fishing enthusiasts, and drifters looking for cheaper lodging.

The day had turned lighter when Fergus and Eva returned to his room and Fred went off to eat downstairs. The saddlebags on the bed appeared untouched.

Dick and Jubal had gone to their own rooms.

"Get some shut-eye," Fergus told Eva.

He reached out and touched her neck. She jerked back.

He grabbed her arm and pulled her back close to him. She threw her head back and he stroked her neck with the tips of his fingers. She shook her head and struggled to free herself.

"You have a purty neck," he said.

"Don't touch me."

Fergus laughed and grinned at her with a gargoyle leer.

"You look a lot like your aunt Eileen," he said. "But you never knew her, did you?"

"No. You killed her. You murdered her."

"It was never proved. She died, yeah, but it was an accident."

"Ma said you murdered her."

"Your ma says a lot of things what ain't true."

"I hate you," she said.

"Aw, go on and get some sleep. You look like you was drug through brush."

She turned away and slumped onto the bed. She was asleep in minutes.

Fergus rummaged through one of his saddlebags and brought out a straight razor and a small mug with a round bar of shaving soap in it. He went to the mirror over a small table with a porcelain basin in it. He poured water from a pitcher into the basin and dipped a shaving brush into it. Then he made lather with the brush in the soap dish and began to spread it on his beard. He glanced over at Eva and saw that she was asleep.

He held the razor up to his throat. He shaved through the lather and paused, looking at the contours of his throat. He moved his head and stretched the muscles of his neck. The razor was sharp. He pressed it into his throat and thought about how easy it would be to just cut his own throat, easier than with the bowie knife.

The thought fascinated him as he stroked his foamy neck

with the razor. He heard the scratch of the bristles as the blade sliced through the stubble. The soapy foam curled up on the razor. He dipped the blade into the water and waggled it until all the foam disappeared. He slanted the razor and continued to scythe the hairs on his neck and chin. When his neck was free of beard, he wiped the patches of soap away with a towel and tilted his head, first to one side, then the other, marveling at the bulge of his Adam's apple and the veins in his skin. He stroked his shaved neck and touched the spot where he could feel his pulse.

A strange sense of excitement washed over him as he remembered Eileen.

She had been naked beneath him on their bed and his hands had begun stroking her delicate throat as they made love. Her eyes were closed until those last moments when his fingers pressed hard into the muscles of her neck. Then they had flown open as she gasped for breath, looking up at him as he tightened his grip and shuddered with sublime pleasure as he brought her to an orgasm. He kept tightening, tightening, until he heard a bone snap in her throat. Her eyes blazed with a final bluish light and she bucked up against him, wheezing out her last breath. He felt a thrill as her eyes turned glassy and closed forever.

He had not been convicted of murder. Instead, he pled guilty to involuntary manslaughter and was sentenced to prison for ten years. He was released after serving four years for good behavior. He laughed to himself at the thought. He had sliced a fellow inmate's throat during that last year, using a straight razor much like the one he was using now, and he could still experience the thrill of seeing the lifeblood spurt from the man's neck as his legs turned rubbery and collapsed. No one had seen him do it, and he had tossed the razor in another man's cell, atop his bunk.

Fergus finished shaving, elated by the memories of those

two deaths. He wiped the blade clean on the towel, folded it up, and returned it to his saddlebag, along with the damp soap and dried mug.

His men returned to his room, looked at the sleeping Eva, and sat down in two chairs and on the divan. Dick carried the saddlebags over to the table, and they began removing the stacks of money, their eyes wide, their tongues licking their dry lips in anticipation of the counting and division.

"I get right at nine thousand dollars," Fred said.

"Ninety-three hunnert," Jubal said, placing a stack of twenty-dollar bills alongside the stacks.

"That's one thousand for each of you," Fergus said. "I'll take the lion's share."

"Fair enough," Jubal said. "You done all the figurin' on this one."

"And I'll figure the next one, too," Fergus said as the men began dividing up the money.

When they were finished, Dick asked Fergus a question that was on all their minds.

"You got somethin' else figured, Fergus?"

"Damned right," Fergus said. The men stuffed money in their saddlebags, holding out enough pocket money to make them all feel rich. Fergus stuffed most of his money in his own saddlebag and slid it between his feet as he sat down on the divan.

The other three men hunched forward to listen to him.

"Longest we'll stay here is three days," Fergus said. "Case Emma shows up in a day or two. Jubal, I'll pay for two more days of roomin', but we ain't goin' to wait any longer for the bitch."

"We ain't?" Jubal said.

"No. We got two banks to hit. You're all goin' to need a gunny sack to carry all your money in afore we're done with this part of the country."

"Where?" Dick asked. "Here in Longmont?"

"First we ride to Greeley, that bank Fred told us about."

"Ain't a bank, really," Fred said. "More like a big old loan office. Easy pickin's."

"That's the one," Fergus said. "The Greeley Savings and Loan. Ain't nobody goin' to catch us neither. You know why?"

The three men all shook their heads.

"Fred says they got a sheriff and one lone deppity. We kill them first, real quick, and then rob the loan office."

"That's real smart," Jubal said. "Shoot both of 'em."

"No gunfire," Fergus said. "Fred says them two fix coffee ever' mornin' and drink it in the jail. We'll walk in like we was lookin' for law advice and grab 'em. I'll slit their throats and we'll go get the money. We'll ride east and circle around, come back to Longmont. By the time they get up a posse, they won't have no tracks to foller."

"Yeah," Fred said, "sounds good."

"They'll be like a chicken with its head cut off," Dick said, chuckling to himself.

"Then, afore we leave Longmont, we do the same here. They ain't but one lawman here and a deppity still wet behind the ears. We stick up the Union Bank and ride out rich as Croesus."

"Who's Croesus?" Jubal said.

"Like King Midas," Dick said.

"Like us, pretty soon," Fergus said. "Now, you all get some shut-eye. We ride to Greeley real early tomorrow."

"What about that girl you got, Fergus? You gonna leave her here?"

"No, she goes with us. Only thing is, she don't get no share of the money."

The men all laughed, shouldered their saddlebags, and left the room.

Fergus walked over and locked the door. He pocketed the key and gave one last glance at Eva before he lay down on the divan.

He threw an arm across his face and closed his eyes.

Yes, he thought, he'd take Eva to Greeley with them, but she wouldn't leave Longmont alive. Neither would Emma.

He unbuckled his gunbelt and let it fall to the floor. He touched the handle of his bowie knife atop his gunbelt, stroked it with a loving hand.

He thought of Eva's young throat, and of Emma's, the pleasure it would give him to open them with the blade of his knife and watch the blood spurt out.

Nothing would give him more pleasure than to see their lives flow away in those beautiful crimson fountains.

A while later, while Fergus slept, it began to rain. He never heard its soft patter against the window panes. In the mountains, on Longs Peak, there would be a fresh dusting of April snow by morning. The air would be fresh and clean after the rain and the sun would be shining. For now, there were only the dark dreams and his saddlebags full of green-back dollars and a horse galloping through a lake of fresh blood.

21

LARIMER STREET SEEMED TO IGNORE CLOCKS. THOUGH DAWN WAS breaking, the streetlamps still glowed yellow, with white halos around the burning gas of their nuclei.

As John, Ben, and Emma rode toward the Larimer Hotel, they heard the strum of guitars, the blare of trumpets, the ring of banjos, and the breathy organ sounds of accordions. To Emma, it felt as if she were riding into another world, a strange world where time had ceased to exist.

At the sight of the Larimer Hotel, Emma's heart quickened. She felt the weariness in her bones, but the thought that Eva might be somewhere inside that clapboard building revived her spirits. She followed Ben and John to the hitchrail out front, stared longingly into the dim-lit windows as if expecting her daughter to appear at any moment and press her pretty face up against the smoky glass.

But the lobby was empty when the three walked inside the hotel. A single lamp glowed on a table between two chairs, the wick turned down low so that it barely beat off the shadows floating in the room like crepe paper crows. The desk was deserted and dark.

John walked to the desk and lifted a small brass bell. He rang it several times, and they waited. He rang it again, and they could hear something rustling beyond the door behind the counter. A moment later, the door squeaked open and an old man, slipping up one strap of his suspenders, emerged. He was carrying a small lamp. He set the lamp on the counter.

"Mornin'," he said, his eyes rheumy behind horn-rimmed glasses, his chin leaking a snowy Vandyke beard, his moustache bone white and flowing like some cuneiform scrawl above his upper lip. He pushed a black-and-red ledger toward John and flipped it open. "Separate rooms? Or one room with two beds and a cot? A dollar for the singles, three for the triple."

Emma stepped up beside John, her face drawn and wan, worry lines around her blue eyes, a wisp of hair dangling over her right cheek.

"Is there a young woman staying here?" she asked. "Thin, with light hair, hair like straw, blue eyes like mine?"

"No, ma'am, not that I've seen. Course, I only been on since midnight and no little kids checked in, far as I know."

"I'm looking for a man who might have that young girl," John said. "He might have left a message for this woman."

"Oh, yes," the clerk said, "they's an envelope in the drawer here."

He slid open a drawer, pulled out a small white envelope. He held it up to his glasses and read the name on it.

"You Mrs. Argus Blanchett?" he said.

"Yes," Emma gasped and snatched the envelope out of the clerk's hands. She tore it open, read it, once, then again. Tears leaked from her eyes. She handed the note to John.

Emma, you come to Longmont. Eva and me will be at the Platte Hotel for a couple of days. You come by yourself. If

*you don't come, you won't see your daughter no more. I
ain't kidding.*

"Bastard," John said under his breath. He handed the
note to Ben.

"When did you get this note?" he asked the clerk while
Ben was reading it.

"Evenin' clerk handed it to me when I come on, a little after midnight. When I come up, I did see some men ride
away and it looked like they might have had a gal with 'em.
Wasn't payin' much attention. My rheumatiz was actin' up
somethin' mean and I forgot and left my cane at home."

"They said they would be staying here, so the man I'm
looking for must be using an alias."

"Wouldn't surprise me none. We got more Smiths and
Browns in the register than you can shake a stick at."

"We'll take three separate rooms," John said. He put a
five-dollar bill on the counter.

"Yes, sir. I'll get your change. Just put your John Henrys
in the book there. Lady can use whatever name she wants,
of course."

Emma picked up the register and scanned the names.
She didn't recognize any of them and set it back down,
signed her name. John and Ben did the same. The clerk gave
him change and set three keys on the table.

"Right next to each other on the second floor," the clerk
said. "So's you won't have to look far to find each other."

There was no innuendo in the man's words. John touched
a forefinger to his hat.

"Much obliged," John said. "You got a livery nearby
where we can put up our horses?"

"Just down the street. Turn right when you step outside.
Stable boy's probably asleep, but they's a wooden box by
the doors where you can put your greenbacks and there
should be stalls open, plenty of hay and grain."

"Thanks," John said. He handed keys to Ben and Emma.

"Let's put the horses up," John said to Ben. "Emma, you can go on up. You look mighty tired."

"I am tired. I'll get my saddlebags and go on up, if you don't mind."

"Sure," John said.

They walked outside. Emma removed her saddlebags and said good night to both men. She looked, John thought, like she was ready to drop. He watched her go inside the hotel and start up the stairs.

"Mighty fine woman," Ben said. "She's got spunk."

"I'm wondering if she'll have the grit to ride to Long-mont tomorrow."

"Haw. You couldn't keep her from it, John. She'd ride to hell for that daughter of hers."

"So would I," John said.

"I reckon I would, too," Ben said.

They walked the horses to the stables down the street beyond all the cantinas and saloons. There were no nearby streetlamps, but they could make out the sign on the false front: LARIMER LIVERY.

"Plain enough," Ben said.

"You want to get folks to find you in a big city like this, you keep it simple," John said.

"Hell, you can smell it a block away."

"Ben, you got a head on your shoulders, all right. Not much gets past you."

"Aw, Johnny. You got the head. All I got is a good nose. 'Specially for horseshit."

Ben swung one of the doors open and they led the horses inside the stable. It was nearly pitch dark, but there were filaments of light streaming through cracks in the boards. The smell was musty, thick with the heavy scents of horse manure, urine, hay, and slobbered-over grain. A couple of the horses crashed against their stalls and whickered at the newcomers. Ben walked along the rows of stalls and opened the doors to the empty ones.

"I'll strip the horses, Johnny, if you can scout up some grain."

"See if there's water in those stalls while you're at it, Ben."

John handed Gent's reins to Ben. He pulled him into an open stall, then closed the door. John walked down the aisle, stepping on straw that gave under his feet and whispered at his heels. He found troughs filled with cracked corn and wheat, a bin full of loose hay, alfalfa from the smell of it, he decided, and buckets hanging from nails on sturdy wooden posts. He filled one with corn, the other with wheat, and walked back down to where Ben was boarding their horses.

"There's water in the stalls," Ben said, "kind of scummy with straw and such. Drinkable."

"You taste it, Ben?"

Ben laughed.

They finished unsaddling their horses, stripping off their bridles. They laid their tack up in a small room with saw-horses, pegs, and shelves, slung their saddlebags over their shoulders, and carried their rifles out of the livery and back onto the street.

"When you figure on riding to Longmont, John?" Ben asked as they walked back to the hotel.

"Fergus has a good start on us. We can't catch up to him. So, we sleep maybe four hours or so, break our fast, and head out in five or six hours."

"I could sleep a week."

"Okay. Part of it will be in the saddle."

"You got a great big heart, Johnny."

"When a man hunts, he doesn't need much sleep."

"Nothing to hunt until we get to Longmont."

"Most of hunting is in the mind, Ben. You look, you listen, you track, and you think. You sleep. I'll hunt."

"John, you're about as much fun as listenin' to the temperance ladies at church."

"Ben, we're facing at least three men we don't know anything about, and one we know to be a cut-throat killer. And they have a young girl with them as a hostage. If we make a mistake, Eva's dead. Fergus is holding most of the cards."

"You got that six-gun, John. It ain't never failed you."

"A six-gun's not always the straight flush or even the high ace."

"No, but it's a royal flush against a knife, to my way of thinkin'."

"You sleep, Ben. I'll do the thinking," John said as they reached the hotel.

"I need eight hours in a featherbed," Ben said.

"Just make sure nobody pours hot tar over you while you're wallowing in chicken feathers."

The two men said good night, unlocked their doors, and went inside their rooms.

As soon as John put his rifle down on the table and draped his saddlebags over the arm of a chair, he felt the weariness assail him, creeping through his bones, sapping his muscles. He sat down and pulled off his boots. His feet felt like alien appendages, soft and tender.

He stripped off his gunbelt and hung it on the bedpost, took off his trousers and left his shirt on. The room was dark, but he could make out the shapes of the table, the bed, the chairs and the stuffed couch, the chest of drawers. There were two lamps in the room, a water pitcher, and a large bowl. He wanted no light. He lay atop the soft comforter and glanced at the window, its panes silvered with moonlight. Strands of music drifted through the open window, a plaintive guitar in a minor key, the soft and mellow tones of a muted trumpet, the thrum of a bass fiddle, and the thump of a rhythmic bass drum.

He closed his eyes and let the night wash over him with its music and its feeble shawl of moon and starlight.

Then he heard a soft knock on his door. For a moment he thought he was imaging it or that he had fallen asleep and was dreaming.

The knocking grew louder.

"Coming," he called out and arose from the bed, padding to the door in his aromatic socks.

He opened the door, and there was Emma, standing there in her pink flannel nightgown, a bundle of folded clothes under one arm.

"May I come in, John?" she whispered.

He nodded and watched her glide across the dark room with all the grace of a queen at court. He closed the door and locked it.

"Are you sure, Emma?" he said as he followed her across the room.

She lay her clothing atop the table, next to his rifle, and turned to him.

"I need you," she said. "I've never felt so lost and alone in my life."

He took her into his arms and held her tightly against him. The scent of her floated up to his nostrils, and he buried his face in her hair. He thought she was going to cry, but she only sighed and wrapped her arms around his waist, squeezed him with surprising strength.

"I think I need you, too, Emma," he said softly. "And I know what it's like to be all alone."

They kissed, and the darkness clasped them to its bosom, held them in a secret grotto where all was peaceful and full of promise, a place where moonlight played on their faces and sparkled in their longing eyes.

22

FERGUS CURSED THE RAIN.

The rain was icy and blew across the trail in crystal sheets, spattering on his slicker with the sound of a thousand drumsticks clattering on a tar paper roof. The wind lashed his face with savage droplets that stung with the ferocity of maddened wasps and burned his eyes as if they were hot sparks flying off a burning log.

Dick was riding in the vanguard since he was the most familiar with the road. He was hunched over his saddle horn, his black slicker sleek as sealskin. An occasional cart pulled by a burro passed them, so Fergus knew they were on the right road. Eva was a small black glob in a slicker Fergus had bought from the hotel clerk, something left long ago in Lost and Found, a child's raincoat that just barely fit the girl. Jubal and Fred followed behind. Fergus could hear their voices grumbling about the rain, even though he couldn't make out the words.

"We ought to wait another day," Fred said as he rode up alongside Fergus. "We can't see shit in this downpour."

"Perfect day to hit the bank, Fred."

"Perfect, my ass. We can't ride fast when we make our getaway."

"You let me worry about that. Nobody's goin' to be chasin' us."

"Damn you, Fergus. You always think you're right."

"That's because I am. Now, quit your bellyachin' and shut up."

"To hell with you, Blanchett." Fred dropped back to complain to Jubal.

Fergus laughed to himself.

"Anything I hate," he said to Eva, "it's a damned whiner."

Eva said nothing. She was shivering, and she felt blisters forming on her buttocks. She was truly saddle sore and miserable, lonesome for her mother and wishing John Savage and Ben Russell would appear out of the darkness and kill her uncle. She had visions of John shooting Fergus out of the saddle. She could see the flame from John's pistol, hear the bullet, and see it split open her uncle's head and knock him to the ground. She kept playing the scene over and over in her mind like those little books you could flip so that the images of the people seemed to run, jump, or dance in quick succession.

An early morning stage passed them in the darkness. The driver waved to them as they all pulled their horses to the side of the road to let the coach pass. The shades of the windows were drawn down tight and there was a tarp over the luggage on top. They were all spattered with mud as the horses splashed on past them, each of the four wearing blinders.

Two wagons full of fresh vegetables passed them, too, the Mexicans grinning at them from wet seats, their serapes pinned under their straw sombreros so that they looked like women wearing large shawls. These events made the time go faster for Fergus, his men, and Eva, but after they had passed by, the road was lonelier and darker than ever, and the wind blew at their backs and made the wheat fields shiver and roll like a tawny sea on both sides of the road. There was a keening in the wind that sounded like the mournful siren sounds of Irish banshees.

They rode into a deserted town just before dawn drained away some of the darkness. Dick rode to the sheriff's office at the end of one main block and dismounted two doors away. He tied his horse to a hitch ring as the others rode up. The light from a lamp in the sheriff's office threw a rectilinear light on the boardwalk, a light laced with silver lances and sparkling droplets of rain.

Fergus dismounted and pulled Eva off her horse. He tied their reins to hitch rings and unbuttoned his slicker so that he could reach his knife and pistol when the time came.

"You stay tight with Jubal, hear?" he told Eva, passing her off to the big man, who loomed up out of the rain like some giant apparition, water dripping from the brim of his hat like a misty veil.

Eva's hair was soaking wet. She squeezed water out of it and ruffled the strands to fluff them up. Jubal put a hand on her shoulder.

"Don't you run or scream, little darlin'," he said.

She turned on him, anger flaring in her eyes.

"Don't talk to me like that," she said. "I'm not your darling."

"Hey, settle down, Miss Eva."

Eva glared and turned away from him.

Fergus and Fred followed Dick into the sheriff's office, sopping across the hardwood floor toward a bench that was pushed against one wall. None of them sat down. The aroma of strong coffee permeated the room, and there was a smell of cigarette and cigar smoke in the bluish haze clinging to the ceiling.

Sheriff Thorsen Brinvald sat at the desk, his feet propped up on one edge. His gunbelt hung on a peg behind his chair, next to a doorless cabinet stacked with rifles and shotguns. A battered coffeepot sat on top of a hot potbellied stove. His deputy, Elmer Toomey, sat in another chair, cradling a cup of coffee in both hands, a hand-rolled cigarette dangling from his thin lips. He wore a pistol and sported a deputy's badge on his black shirt with thin red stripes. The sheriff wore suspenders and made up in girth what Toomey lacked in bulk.

Fat sheriff, thin deputy, Fergus thought, his eyes measuring both men as he doffed his dripping hat.

"Well, what brings you folks in here so early? Stage to Denver's already left. There's one leaving for Cheyenne around noon."

The deputy looked at Eva, bedraggled Eva, in her ill-fitting slicker and with her long hair drenched to a sodden mass.

"Where's your mama, missy?" Toomey said. He set his cup down on a table where the lamp burned and took his cigarette out of his mouth.

Eva just stood there, voiceless.

"Now," Fergus said as he put his hat back on his head.

Dick and Fred drew their pistols and walked to the sheriff. Jubal's pistol appeared in his hand. He strode to Deputy Toomey and put the barrel square against the man's forehead. He reached down and snatched the lawman's pistol from its holster and threw it behind him on the floor.

"What the hell . . ." Brinvald said as Fred and Dick braced him on either side. They lifted the sheriff from his chair and poked the barrels of their pistols into the ring of fat on both sides.

"What's goin' on?" Toomey asked as Jubal cocked his pistol. "I ain't got but two or three dollars in my pocket."

"Shut up," Fergus said. He drew the bowie knife from its scabbard and walked over to the deputy. Jubal stepped aside, but kept his cocked pistol pressed against Toomey's forehead.

Toomey cringed backward in his chair. The cigarette dropped from his hand and hissed in a puddle of water where Jubal had stood a moment before.

Fergus shot his left arm out and grabbed a shock of Toomey's hair. He pushed his head back, stepped in close and with a single swipe of his blade, slashed a deep cut in the deputy's throat. He did it so fast that Toomey had no chance to cry out. There was only a startled look of fear in his eyes before blood spurted from the gash in his neck. His legs twitched and he slumped dead in his chair, blood spurting from his neck like a gushing fountain. His shirt and badge turned dark with crimson streaks.

"My God," the sheriff gasped. "What'd you do that for?"

Brinvald looked dazed, like a man in a trance. He wore a stupefied look on his face as he stared at the lifeless body of his deputy.

"Grab him, Dick," Fergus said. "Bring him to me, you and Fred."

Dick and Fred grabbed the sheriff's arms and hustled him from behind his desk. The sheriff struggled, tried to free himself, but both men held him tight.

They held Brinvald fast as Fergus stepped up to him and looked into the sheriff's tortured eyes. He saw the fear in them and smiled.

"Wha-what are you going to do?" Brinvald gasped,

shrinking back from Fergus as if a few inches of distance could save him from a horrible and swift death.

"You're too fat, Sheriff," Fergus said and jabbed the point of his knife straight into Brinvald's Adam's apple, twisting the blade and then slicing first one way, then the other, until there was a gaping hole in the man's neck and blood spurted a half foot. The sheriff's legs collapsed beneath him and the two men let him go. He pitched forward into a pool of blood. A last gust of air issued from the rip in his throat, and then he made no more sound and did not move.

"Drag them back into the jail," Fergus said. "And, Jubal, you sop up some of this blood. We got to wait a while for the bank to open."

Fergus swiped the blade of his knife on his trousers, slipped it back in its sheath. He walked over to Eva who was holding her hands in front of her face. Her eyes were squeezed tightly shut, and she was trembling.

"There, there, Eva," Fergus said. "It's all over."

Eva kept her eyes shut and held her hands over her face. She could hear a door open and the sound of a man being dragged through it and into another room. Jubal holstered his pistol and lifted the dead deputy by the shoulders and dragged him out of the room.

Eva heard the clank of a cell door closing and some rustling beyond the door. She knew what her uncle Fergus had done, but she had watched none of it. She retreated into that dark place of imaginings where she could seek out John Savage and pray that he would appear and shoot all these men and take her back to the mountains with him. In her mind, all things were possible, but she knew that if she opened her eyes, there was no hope that John Savage or her mother would walk into the jail and rescue her.

"Sit down, Eva," Fergus said and pulled on her arm. He sat down and she sat beside him.

"I want to go home," she pleaded, her hands still covering her face.

"We'll see your mama in Longmont," he said. "Then, maybe, you can go home."

The men returned and started wiping up blood from the floor with towels they found in a cabinet.

"Get some cups, Jubal, and pour us all some coffee. And somebody pull the shades on them front windows."

"I'll make us some fresh coffee," Fred said. "There's enough cups to go around."

Dick pulled the shades on the front window. Then he locked the front door.

In the silence, they could hear the rain on the roof and pattering against the front windowpanes. Daylight seeped around the edges of the shades as the sun cleared the horizon and ascended into bulging black clouds. The light turned gray and feeble as if to keep the town locked into a mood of desolation and hopelessness. There were no people to be seen on the streets at that hour.

The smell of fresh coffee did not diminish the feeling of isolation that Eva felt when she opened her eyes and saw the faint light at the edges of the windows. She felt as if she had entered a ghost town, a town where all the people were dead and if she screamed at the top of her voice, no one would hear her except the ugly men who held her prisoner.

23

BARNEY INGERSOL DROVE STAGECOACH FOR THE ROCKY MOUNT Overland from Denver to Pueblo and back and from Greeley to Denver. Sometimes he drove the stage to Cheyenne. But the company was located in Denver, which was the hub of the RMO. When he encountered the four riders and the young girl on horseback on his way to Longmont from whence he would drive the team to Denver, he remarked to his shotgunner, Dewey Macklin: "See them folks?"

"Sure did," Dewey said.

"Third time's a charm, Dew."

"Eh?"

"That's the third time we've run acrost them riders," Barney said. "You recollect?"

Ingersol was in his early forties, a robust man with strong muscular arms and sturdy legs. He wore a light sheepskin jacket and a weathered gray Stetson that matched his gray muslin shirt. Dewey was a mite older, nearing fifty, with a face covered with scraggly red-and-black hair, a pork-pie checkered hat, two Colts on his gunbelt, a faded blue cotton shirt, galluses, and striped gray trousers tucked into high-topped work boots. He carried a sawed-off Greener loaded with double-ought buck, and chewed the stub of a cheroot he never lit.

"Seems like we seen them same riders before, Barney," Dewey said. "Seems like it was dark, then, too."

"That's right. This is the third time we done seen that same little gal and maybe one or two of the same riders."

"Yep, seems like we seen her before. Same dress. Only this time she was wearin' a black slicker. You could see her dress, though."

"Don't it seem strange to you?"

"How so?"

"I mean that same little old gal a-ridin' in the dark, some-times with two men and sometimes with four."

"It's somethin' to ponder over, for sure, Barney."

"We saw her when we was comin' from Pueblo, and I saw 'em ridin' down Larimer Street the other night, and now we seen 'em again, headin' toward Greeley."

"Yep. Mighty peculiar, you ask me."

"Mighty peculiar. They ain't messengers."

"No, I reckon they ain't. But they sure cover a lot of ground."

"Kinda spooky, Dew."

"Yep."

The stage rode through the rain and into Longmont, where they picked up two passengers going to Denver when the sun was standing full in the sky, lighting up the fresh snow on Longs Peak and the other mountains in the front range.

There, while Barney checked the traces and examined the hooves of the four horses, the Bobbitt Freight Lines wagon pulled up to the stage stop and the driver, Oren Pir-tle, threw down a stack of newspapers bound together by manila twine. Pirtle glanced over at the stagecoach and hailed Barney.

"Old man Bobbitt was kilt last night," he said.

"Earl?"

"Yep, his missus and both boys, too. They's a big headline in this mornin's *Rocky Mountain News*. Take a look."

Oren pulled away, headed for Greeley. Barney walked over, cut the twine, and picked up the tabloid from Denver.

He read the headline in seventy-two-point Bodoni Bold:
BOBBITT FAMILY MURDERED.

Barney saw that the paper was an Extra edition. He beckoned to Dewey and started reading the story that appeared under the byline Charles Perlee:

Sometime after midnight, Constable Harvey Lee Root was summoned to the home of Earl Bobbitt, owner of Bobbitt Freight Lines in Denver. There, a neighbor showed him the bodies of Earl Bobbitt, his wife, Anella, and sons, Phillip and Jerome. All were dead, their throats cut. Root told this reporter that an empty safe was found in an upstairs bedroom where Mr. Bobbitt kept his money and valuables. The safe was empty and Mr. Root does not know how much money was taken. He said that a witness, who did not wish to be identified, claimed that four men and a young girl were seen riding away from the Bobbitt house shortly after the murders occurred.

There was more to the story, but Barney handed the paper to Dewey, who read it hurriedly, then put it back atop the stack. A clerk at the stage stop came out and picked up the papers and carried them inside. He, too, was avidly reading the lurid news story.

"Well, that's it, then," Barney said to Dewey.

"What's it?" Dewey asked.

"That solves the mystery about them four horsemen and the young gal."

"You think it's the same ones what murdered Earl and his family?"

"Damned right I do. Plain as the nose on your face, Dew. Them four was highwaymen, pure and simple."

"What about the young gal?"

"Probably a lookout. Or bait."

"Bait?"

"Yeah, you know. She probably showed up at Earl's door and begged for food or something. When he come to the door, them robbers overpowered him and made him open his safe."

"I heard old Earl kept a lot of money out to his house."

"Yeah, me, too."

"You better tell somebody that we seen them highwaymen just this mornin'."

"I will. Soon as we get to Denver."

"No, you better tell the sheriff here in Longmont. They must have come through here."

"Well, you go see if Sheriff Lucas is in his office and tell him what we seen. I'll meet you there."

The sheriff's office was just a few doors down the street. Sheriff Isaac Lucas was releasing an overnight drunk from his jail when Dewey burst into his office. He told him about the story in the newspaper, then recounted what he and Barney had discussed about the four men and a young girl.

"We think it's the same ones, and they was ridin' toward Greeley early this mornin'."

"Might be I seen them folks over at the Platte," Lucas said. He was a tall, string bean of a man with a face that looked as if it had been carved with a hatchet—thin straight nose, straight jawlines and chiseled cheekbones, a curlicue of a mouth under a thin black moustache. He carried a .38 Smith & Wesson on his gunbelt and wore crisply ironed trousers and a pale blue chambray shirt with a silver star pinned to his left shirt pocket. He was forty-two years old and afflicted with a mild case of rheumatism that made him limp slightly. His legs were bowed from years in the saddle, running cattle up to Texas from Mexico, and from Texas to Colorado and Wyoming. He had been sheriff of Longmont for only two months and knew very little about the law.

"We got to get on to Denver, Isaac. I hope you catch them jaspers."

"I don't have no deputy," Lucas said. "Be hard for me to open the ball against four desperadoes."

"Get you a Greener like I got," Dewey said and ran outside as the stagecoach pulled up in front of Lucas' office.

"I got me a scattergun, twelve gauge," Lucas said. But the coach was already moving and Dewey looked like a fly crawling up a wall as he pulled himself up on the side of the coach.

"You tell him, Dew?"

"I told him, Barney. I don't think Lucas is much interested."

"Maybe they'll send out a posse from Denver." He snapped the reins across the horses' backs, and the coach lurched toward Denver. Fluffy white clouds began to populate the blue sky, and there were wisps of cotton forming from the moisture left by the overnight rain. The mountains stood out like sculptured monuments, their snowy mantles shining like beacons. The air smelled fresh, and there was a fragrance of wildflowers floating aloft from the prairie.

The horses blew steam from their nostrils and their rippling muscles tautened the traces as they galloped toward Denver.

The wheels of the coach churned through light mud and puddles of water, leaving ruts that marked their passing, spewing out daubs of mud and trickles of dirty water behind the rear boot. The passengers inside, a drummer and a tinhorn gambler, held on to the straps for dear life, rocking back and forth on separate seats like full-sized targets at a carnival shooting booth. The gambler uncorked a bottle of rotgut whiskey, took a swallow, and passed it to the drummer.

He took a drink and held the bottle up to the light. Small dark particles floated in the liquid.

"This is probably a lot more beneficial than the snake oil I sell," he said.

"Hell, first time I drunk some of that, I thought it was snake oil," the gambler said.

"Here's to your health," the drummer said, taking another sip.

The coach rumbled on for hours until one of the wheels struck a rock. Some of the spokes snapped with a sound like rifle shots. The coach lurched and sank to one side as the wheel wobbled and canted to an acute angle just as Barney pulled hard on the reins and stopped the horses. He set the brake and looked down at the twisted, broken wheel.

"We got work to do," he said to Dewey. "Put away that Greener and give me a hand."

Dewey lay the shotgun down at his feet.

"This don't auger well, Barney," he said, just before he climbed down.

"No, it sure as hell don't," Barney said, marking the sun's arc in the sky. They had been making good time and were only an hour out of Denver.

They were also out in the middle of nowhere and the road was deserted for miles in both directions. A pair of turkey buzzards wheeled in the sky and, in the distance, a small band of pronghorns galloped across the prairie, their white rumps flashing in the afternoon sunlight.

24

FERGUS STOOD AT THE WINDOW OF THE SHERIFF'S OFFICE IN Greeley, watching the street outside as the sun shot light through the rain and the outlines of the buildings slowly arose out of the darkness and took on defined shapes, colors, and names. There was the Crawford Café a few doors down, lamplight yellowing its windows, Olsen's Hardware Store, with its gypsum-painted sign atop an adobe front, and Reed's Sporting Goods & Sundries, with its high false front as if to outdo the other establishments.

He watched as people flocked to the café, ranchers on horseback, Mexicans with carts loaded with woven blankets, clay jars, and kiln-baked plates, ashtrays, cups, and saucers, and other business people alighting from buggies and wagons to break their fasts and wake themselves up with fresh hot coffee.

On the corner, just barely visible, he saw the white building that was the Greeley Savings & Loan. Its windows were dark and opaque, with only a glint of sunlight to reveal that they were glass, and the curtains were pulled.

"What time does that loan office open, Dick?" Fergus asked as he turned away from the window.

"Around nine, I reckon."

Fergus glanced up at the Waterbury on the wall. He frowned.

"A good two hours to wait," he said.

"Man opens up a little before nine," Dick said. "He opens the curtains and lets the clerks in when they knock on the front door. Two men. One young, one a little older."

"They pack iron?"

"No," Dick said. "Around ten, there's a guard comes on. He wears some kind of uniform. Has a peashooter on his Sam Browne belt. Looks like a .32 Smith. He's about fifty, I guess, and stinks like a rum pot. He carries a flask in his hip pocket and gets himself a cup of coffee from the little room next to the president's office. Takes him twenty minutes or so to take up his station by the front door. He stands there, grinning like a shit-eating dog at the customers who come in."

"So, we don't have to worry about him," Fergus said.

"The vault will be open about nine fifteen and, if there's a bunch of folks, the two tellers will be at the windows. The gate to where they are isn't locked or nothin'. You can just push right through."

"See any guns anywhere?"

"Naw. I figure the president's got one in his desk drawer. I filled out a loan application in his office and didn't see no gun case."

"I'll go in first," Fergus said. "I'll ask about a loan, and they should let me see the president. Give me five minutes, then the rest of you come in and brace the clerks. No shoot-

ing if we can help it. We'll get all the money we can and
light a shuck for Longmont."

"It should go smooth," Dick said.

"It better go smooth," Fergus said.

They waited and drank coffee and some chewed on
jerky. Jubal took Eva to the outhouse out in back of the jail,
and the men relieved themselves in the corner of one of the
cells.

A little before nine a.m. Fergus left the jail and walked
toward the bank. Moments later, the others left, one by one,
and took up stations next to the bank.

The bank manager had already entered the building and
then let in the two clerks before Fergus entered the bank.

The clerks were all smiles as he approached the counter.
Their cages were open. Both men wore armbands and were
neatly combed and groomed.

"I came in to apply for a loan on my farm," Fergus said.

"Yes, sir," one of the clerks said. "I'll see if Mr. Ralston
can see you right away."

The clerk went into the president's office. Fergus saw
Ralston look up and nod to the clerk, who turned on his heel
and walked back to the counter.

"If you'll just come inside, Mr. Ralston will see you,
sir."

The clerk pointed to the gate. Fergus went through it
and entered Ralston's office. Ralston stood up and extended
his hand.

"I'm Willard Ralston," the manager said. "Mister . . . ?"

"Dagney," Fergus said. "Herb Dagney."

"Have a seat, Mr. Dagney," Ralston said and sat down
behind his desk.

Fergus sat down and sized up the bank president. He was
a personable young man with black hair slicked down and
parted in the middle. He wore a white shirt and string tie, a

plain corduroy vest with pencils sticking out of the pockets. His smile was irritating to Fergus. It looked pasted on.

Ralston didn't look up when Fergus's men entered the bank. He was pulling forms from his drawers when Dick, Fred, Jubal, and Eva came in the front door. Fergus drew his pistol when Ralston sat up straight.

"What's this?" Ralston said.

"Keep your hands where I can see 'em," Fergus said, "and get up. You and me are going to the vault."

"You can't do this," Ralston said. But he got up from his chair and walked around to get his belly punched in by the barrel of Fergus's pistol.

"Just do what I tell you and nobody will get hurt," Fergus said. "Open the vault."

"I—I—this is outrageous," Ralston said. He doubled over when Fergus jabbed him again with his pistol. He walked to the vault and opened it. There was a shelf with some empty canvas bags on it. They were neatly folded.

"Start putting greenbacks in them bags," Fergus ordered.

He turned for a second to see how his men were doing. Dick and Fred were cleaning out the tellers' drawers, stuffing money into large feed sacks they had brought with them. Jubal and Eva were outside the tellers' cages. Jubal held a gun on two patrons who were plastered against the wall, their hands raised, their faces drawn, their eyes bulging out of their sockets in pure terror.

Ralston was shaking as he put stacks of bills in the leather and canvas bags.

"That's all there is," he said when he had filled two bags.

"Now, sit down, facing the wall and stay there," Fergus said. He grabbed both bags and shut the vault door on the banker. He walked out through the tellers' cages.

"Let's go," he said to the others.

"Boy, we got a pile," Fred said.

"Move," Fergus ordered.

They were all out of the bank and loping to their horses. Nobody followed them. Fergus and Jubal started filling saddlebags with stacks of greenbacks. Fred and Dick stuffed their sacks into their saddlebags. Fergus threw the canvas bags onto the wet and muddy street.

They rode out of town at an easy pace. There was no one to chase them.

Nobody did.

25

THE NEWSBOY OUTSIDE THE LARIMER WAS HAWKING EXTRA editions of the *Rocky Mountain News*. John, Emma, and Ben were just leaving for Longmont. Their horses were saddled and waiting at the hitchrail. John saw the headlines and walked over after he slid his rifle in its scabbard and secured his saddlebags to Gent.

"Family murdered in Cherry Hills. Read all about it! Get your paper with all the gory details. Extra, extra."

John gave the boy a nickel and told him to keep the change.

"Thank you, mister," the boy said and continued walking slowly down Larimer Street.

Ben and Emma came over as John was reading the article. They flanked him and both read the story on the Bobbitt murders.

The blue sky was filling up with vaporous wisps as the morning sun drew dew and rain off the land. Denver had only gotten a smattering of rain during the night and the air was clean and fresh as the trio mounted their horses and rode out of town, heading north to Longmont.

Emma still looked radiant, John thought, as he looked over at her as she rode alongside him. Ben lagged behind a few lengths, his eyes still hooded under the brim of his hat. His beard itched and he was still half asleep, although they had eaten a quick breakfast of hen fruit, sliced apples, buttered toast, and sausages, all downed with strong hot coffee. He was just tired and wondered why John and Emma looked like a couple of spring chickens, full of vim and vigor when he felt as if he had been tarred and feathered during the night on the hard hotel bed.

The two were still talking in those low, intimate tones as they had at breakfast, and he wondered if the two had slept together. None of his business, of course, but they acted like they were married, and he hadn't seen no justice of the peace at the hotel.

The blue sky was strewn with fluffy white clouds, little scraps attaching to larger ones, cirrus strands blending into cumulus forms as if a new cycle of condensation and convection was beginning in order to reinvigorate the earth with more rain later in the week.

"It was beautiful last night, Emma," John said.

"Umm, yes. So beautiful. What you gave me was wonderful. I'm still glowing inside."

"And outside, too."

He never would have expected such a quiet woman as Emma to possess such lust. She had been a wild tigress during the night—insatiable, yet tender and loving as a kitten in the soft embrace of its mother. He didn't know how much of her passion was due to worry over Eva and how much was generated from his own ardent touches and caresses. She had surprised him, and he realized both now and then how little he knew about women.

They kept their voices low and glanced at each other, their faces laden with more meaning than their words. He wanted to reach out and hold her hand but knew that would spark a lot of kidding from Ben. The two were silent until they spotted the stagecoach by the side of the road.

"Oh, look," Emma exclaimed.

"I see it," John said.

"Broke wheel," Ben added as they rode up close.

Barney Ingersol stood over Dewey Macklin, who was setting a wooden spoke into the wheel.

"Howdy," he said to John as he rode up.

"Howdy. Need any help?"

"Nope, Dewey's got that last spoke about set. You folks heading for Longmont? We just come from there this mornin'."

"We are. We're looking for four men and a young girl," John said.

"The Bobbitt thing," Barney said. "It was in the paper this morning."

"Yes," John said.

"We seen 'em. A passel of times."

"When? Where?"

"Last time when we was headin' out from Greeley. They was ridin' in the dark when we passed 'em. We saw the paper in Longmont. Knowed it was the same ones we seen in Denver."

Dewey finished attaching the new spoke to the broken wheel and looked up at Barney.

"Give me a hand, will ya?" Dewey said. "Then we can roll on to Denver."

"Sure," Barney said and bent down to take one side of

the wheel. They attached it to the hub and Dewey drove the shim into the shaft.

"Ready to roll," Dewey said, stepping back as he pumped the handle of the jack and lowered the coach.

He looked up at Savage. "Say," he said, "what you aim to do with them outlaws, anyway?"

"That young woman you saw is my daughter," Emma said. "Those men kidnapped her."

"We wondered what a young gal like that was doin' with a bunch what murdered the Bobbitts."

Dewey put the jack away in the rear boot and climbed up on the seat, picked up his shotgun, and lay it across his lap.

"We think we might find that bunch in Longmont," John said as Barney turned away to walk to the other side of the coach and climb aboard.

"Well, they was headin' for Greeley when we last saw 'em, so they could be way out yonder on the prairie, maybe headin' for Kansas City."

"Thanks, old-timer," John said.

Barney took his seat and picked up the reins. He looked down at John.

"If you catch 'em, what are you aimin' to do, young feller?"

"Get her daughter back, for one thing."

"Well, that might not be too easy. It's four to three, the way I figger it."

"We'll just have to play out the hand," John said.

"Look up the sheriff in Longmont, Isaac Lucas. He might be able to help you some."

"Thanks."

"If you get the young gal away from them jaspers, then what?" Barney's hand gripped the brake, but he didn't release it just yet.

"I may have to put some lights out," John said. "Depends on whether or not those men want to live."

"You sound pretty sure of yourself, young feller."

John patted the butt of his pistol.

"Sure as shootin'," John said.

Barney cracked a grin and released the break.

"Haw," he yelled and snapped the reins across the team's backs. The coach lurched and rolled away, its wheels spitting out gobbets of mud. Dewey lifted his arm and waved. The coach got smaller and smaller until it was just a dot on the horizon, disappearing into a blue sky dotted with puffs of small white clouds.

"Do you think Fergus is heading for Kansas City, John?" Emma asked when they were moving again.

"He told you to meet him in Longmont," John said. "I don't know why he was going to Greeley, but my bet is he'll return to Longmont and wait for you. He's probably there now."

"Oh, I hope so," she said, and he saw tears slip from her eyes and trickle down her cheek in crystal-clear droplets. He felt a tug at his heart. She was so beautiful and the look on her face was so sad. He couldn't bear to dash her hopes, but he knew they were outnumbered, and as long as Fergus had Eva, he was in control. She was the ace in his deck of cards.

If there was shooting, he thought, Eva could be killed in the crossfire. Or worse, if Fergus thought he could no longer use Eva as a bargaining chip, he might just cut her throat to spite Emma.

If he did that, John said to himself, Fergus Blanchett would have a very short life.

Vengeance would not be the Lord's, but John's. But Emma would be broken. She might never recover if her daughter was murdered in such a brutal way. He vowed to prevent that at all costs. Eva deserved to live out her life and so did Emma.

He looked over at her as she wiped her cheeks with her sleeve. It was difficult to reconcile the way she looked just then with the way she had been during the night. She was even more mysterious than he would have imagined. All women had their secrets, he decided, and despite growing closer to Emma, she was still a big mystery to him.

Her allure was drawing him closer to her in many ways, but he knew she would always remain a woman of mystery to him. She had so much passion in her heart, but as he looked at her, none of it was detectable. He saw only a grim-faced mother determined to rescue her daughter.

In such a situation, Emma was probably as dangerous as Fergus and the men who rode with him. He saw the look on her face when he glanced at her again.

There was no sign of that passion she had shown him during the night. No sign, either, of a killer. But just as a she-bear would kill to protect her cubs, he had no doubt Emma would kill Fergus if he harmed a hair on Eva's head.

"Four against three," John murmured to himself.

"Did you say something, John?" Emma asked.

"No, nothing. I was just thinking."

But Ben heard John, and he knew what his friend was thinking.

However, Ben didn't know what John meant. He was sure, though, that he would find out, by and by.

26

ISAAC LUCAS WALKED DOWN THE STREET TO THE SILVER QUEEN saloon. He carried four badges in his pocket and four five-dollar bills he had taken from his safe in the sheriff's office, fine money that he could use at his discretion.

He walked through the batwing doors to the sound of men's voices, the clink of glasses and the whick-whisper of cards being shuffled and dealt. There was also the clink of stacked silver dollars on the green felt card tables.

Men lined the bar, standing and sitting, drinking beer and whiskey. The smell of cigar and cigarette smoke wafted to his nostrils, mingling with the scent of alcohol. The barkeep, Larry Moon, looked up at Lucas as the sheriff strode to the end of the bar, stopping short to face the room.

"Hey, Isaac, you startin' early?" Moon said as he walked to the end of the bar, clutching a towel in his left hand. His white apron was soiled, and he had the stub of an unlit cigar in his pudgy mouth. Heavy eyebrows over a square, chis-eled face gave him the look of a brooding bulldog with his oversized head and balding pate. His belly preceded him by at least six inches.

"No, Larry, I got somethin' to say. Bang something on the bar to quiet everybody down."

"Sure, Isaac. It's too damned noisy in here anyways."

Moon walked back to the cash register and picked up a small wooden bat he used sometimes to break up fights in the bar. He banged it several times on the bar top, startling several of the patrons who were engrossed in conversation.

"Here, here," Moon yelled, "let's have some quiet in here. Sheriff Lucas has got somethin' to say."

The room filled with grumbles and whispers, then fell silent.

Lucas took a step forward.

"Gents," he said, holding up four silver stars in his left hand, spread out like a hand of cards, "I need four men to deputize for a day or so. Job pays five dollars. I want you sober and armed."

Voices rose up all around the room, questioning.

Lucas silenced them by patting the air with both hands, his arms extended.

He had heard some of the questions. The men wanted to know who he was after.

"All I know is that four men and a young gal rode through here early this mornin' headed for Greeley. They murdered Earl Bobbitt and his family. Yeah, that's right, the Bobbitt what owns the freight-haulin' company in Denver. They might come back through here, but we're ridin' toward Greeley to make sure. Might not anything happen, but if we run into them, I need four men to back my hand. You can either sit here and drink your rum, or you can ride with me and earn five bucks to spend on the glitter gals this evenin'."

Chairs scraped on the hardwood floor and men rose

up and rushed toward Lucas, waving their arms, hitching up their gunbelts.

"All right," Lucas said. "I'll pick four of you, the ones I know can shoot. Can't take but four."

There were a dozen men around him in a semicircle.

"Pete, you'll do," he said to Pete Crawford, a man in his thirties and down on his luck. "Slim, you'll do. Hank, step up here, and let's see . . ."

He looked at the other men. One who was shorter than the rest moved to the front.

"Okay, Shorty, you can be a deputy for the day. That's it, gents. Thanks to you all. I got the men I need."

The rejected ones slouched back to their chairs while those at the bar looked on at the small assemblage surrounding Lucas.

Lucas pinned stars on the shirts of the four men.

"Now, raise your right hands. Your right hand, Shorty."

Shorty switched hands from his left to his right.

"I hereby deputize you men to follow my orders and uphold the law. Agreed?"

"Agreed," the men chorused.

"Now, let's get our horses and ride toward Greeley," Lucas said. He turned to the barkeep, who still held the bat in his hands.

"Thanks, Larry. You can have your noise back."

"Thanks a lot, Isaac. You're all heart."

The men followed Lucas out of the saloon. Slim, whose real name was Percy Tutwiler, strode up alongside Lucas.

"When do we get the five dollars, Isaac?"

"Whenever I've got those fellers locked up, Slim."

"Shit, that could take days."

"I'll make it right with you all if it takes longer than a day."

Slim cracked a smile.

"That's mighty sweet talk to my ears, Isaac."

The sun was bright and the men pulled down the brims of their hats as they rode toward Greeley. One or two pulled their rifles from their scabbards and levered a round of .30-caliber ammunition into the firing chambers. They put the rifles on half cock and slid them back into their sheaths. They rode for an hour before Shorty called out.

"I see some riders up ahead. Little black squiggles way down the road."

Lucas stood up in his stirrups. He could barely make out the clump of dark shapes approaching. It was hard to tell if there were more than two riders.

"Keep a sharp eye," he called to the others.

The riders drew closer and when they fanned out, Lucas counted four men on horseback and a small figure in a flapping dress on another horse. The young gal, he thought.

"Don't nobody shoot less'n I say so," Lucas told his men.

"You gonna talk them into the hoosegow, Sheriff?" Larry said.

"The law's the law. I got to give 'em a chance to surrender."

The riders drew closer, their bodies and their horses growing larger and larger. The sun was behind them and cast their shadows in long, ominous globs on the road. They seemed in no hurry, nor did they have guns in their hands. Lucas sucked in a breath and let it out slow. He let his right hand drop to his side so that his pistol was within easy reach. He calculated the distance in his mind and the way his hand would move to grasp the grip and pull the weapon from his holster.

The two groups of riders met. They reined up and confronted each other.

"You're takin' up a lot of road, Sheriff," Fergus said, looking straight at Lucas.

"And them badges are shinin' right in our eyes," Jubal said.

"I'm going to ask you men to surrender quietly so's I can take you back to Longmont and ask you all some questions."

There was a long, empty silence.

"Well, now, Sheriff, you're askin' a whole hell of a lot from peaceable men enjoyin' a mornin' ride."

"You're wanted for murder in Denver, I'm thinkin'," Lucas said.

"You got a warrant?" Fergus asked.

"Don't need one. I got suspicion and that's the letter of the law."

"Oh, it is, is it? Well, here's what I think of your fucking law." Fergus drew his pistol and, as if it were a signal, his men drew theirs. It all happened so fast, Lucas only twitched his hand. It never reached the butt of his pistol.

Fergus cocked his pistol and held it at arm's length. He sighted down the barrel and shot Lucas square in the middle of his chest. Lucas dropped from his saddle like a sack of meal, blood spurting from a hole in his breastbone. The other deputies clawed for their rifles and pistols as Jubal, Dick, and Fred picked out targets and started emptying saddles.

Explosions boomed and orange flames spewed from pistol barrels. Shorty caught a lead round in the throat. Shorty's head burst into bloody mush as his skull blew apart with a .45 slug that collapsed his forehead and blew a saucer-sized hole in the back of his head, spewing brains out in a crimson mist.

Slim got his rifle out and was bringing it to his shoulder when Fred's .44 ripped into his gut and doubled him over.

He dropped his rifle and screamed. A second shot struck him just below his throat, and he belched out a torrent of blood before he toppled sideways and fell to the ground.

Hank drew his pistol and was just cocking it when Dick's bullet shattered his nose and tore off half of his face. His pistol slipped from his hand and he tried to yell, but blood spurted from his nostrils and his eyes glazed over as his brains drowned in blood. The bullet nicked his spine and he stiffened into a barely breathing corpse as he toppled from the saddle.

Pete got off a shot before both Jubal and Fergus fired point-blank into his midsection. The bullets entered from different angles and ripped through his guts and mangled the lower half of his right lung. Pete's shot went high as he toppled backward over the cantle of his saddle, blood gushing from his mouth in a torrent, like red barn paint, little scraps of lung matter mixed in with it like boiled noodles. He twisted and fell to the ground as his horse jumped from under him in a stiff-legged bolt of energy.

Pete writhed on the ground until Dick rode up and shot him in the head. He twitched once and lay still, blood no longer pumping through the holes in his torso.

"Make sure they're all dead," Fergus said as he slid his pistol back in its holster.

Jubal rode up to each fallen man and fired a round into his head.

"They're all plumb dead," he told Fergus.

Fergus turned to Eva, who was staring at the distant mountains in a state of shock, her face drained of color, her eyes wide in an empty stare.

"See what happens when the law comes after your uncle, Eva?" he said.

Eva was frozen into silence, a bewildered expression

on her face, eyes fixed on an empty space far beyond the mountains.

"Let's ride," Fergus said. "Jubal, you keep an eye on little Eva."

"By God, I need a drink," Dick said. He reloaded his pistol from cartridges in his gunbelt.

"Me, too," Fred said. "What's the name of that place in Longmont?"

"The Silver Queen," Dick said. "I've had a few in there."

"My throat's plumb parched, too, Fergus," Jubal said. "How's about we all go in and spend some of this money we got."

"Not a good idea," Fergus said. "I got to keep an eye out for Emma."

"Well, I'm gonna get me a drink," Fred said.

"Me, too," Dick said. "This money's burnin' a hole in my pocket for damned sure."

Jubal looked at Fergus, who made no comment.

"Well, what's the good of havin' all this money if we can't spend none of it," Jubal said. He thrust out his chin in a belligerent act of defiance.

"Suit yourselves," Fergus said. "Just keep your mouths shut and don't drink too damned much. Likely the whole town knows about us now."

"Well, they don't have no sheriff no more," Jubal said as he coaxed Eva to get her horse moving.

"I'd like a drink, too," Eva said. The others turned to her in surprise. Fergus's mouth dropped open.

"Well, now," he said. "A drink might go down just fine after a bloody morning like this. We'll all go to the Silver Queen and maybe celebrate some."

Dick, Fred, and Jubal all let out a cheer.

Eva flashed a wan smile at her uncle before he turned away.

Maybe, she thought, *they'll all get drunk and I can run away.*

It was a dim, slender hope, but it was all she had. Her stomach was filled with revulsion at what she had seen that morning and before that. It swarmed with the fluttering wings of insects and boiled with bile that threatened to erupt upward into her throat.

She really did need a drink, she told herself.

27

IT WAS LATE AFTERNOON WHEN JOHN, BEN, AND EMMA WATERED their horses in the Saint Vrain River just out of Longmont. They stood and watched the train chugging along toward Denver, its coal cars full, smoke from its stack trailing a long gray plume behind it, the little red caboose bringing up the rear, a man waving to them from the top window.

"That stage line won't last much longer, I'm thinkin'," Ben said. "It'll go the way of the buffalo on these plains."

"Maybe the horse will be next," Emma said, patting her horse's neck. "That will be a sad day."

John said nothing. He stared at the massive face of Longs Peak, freshly mantled in snow, and thought of how long the mountains had been there, how much they had seen over the centuries. The mountains seemed to be impervious to man's exploits, his follies, and his bloodthirsty ways. There was no longer a threat of Indians on the plains, but the white men were far more deceitful and treacherous than any red man.

"Not far to go, John," Ben said as he climbed back in the saddle. "You ready?"

John sighed. "I'm ready," he said.

"You thinkin' gold up in them mountains yonder?"

"No. I was just thinking how small and insignificant we are when compared to those majestic rocky mountains."

"Why, John," Emma said, "you have the heart of a poet."

John laughed. "I have my moments," he said and pulled Gent away from the river and put a foot in his stirrup.

"Most men don't think about such things," Emma said as they took to the road. They could see the flour mill rising above the town, the dim shapes of buildings and houses sprawled over a square mile or so, the farms and fields, the tops of fruit trees, and the glint of water in the irrigation ditches.

"They ought to," John said. "The mountains are permanent. We are not."

"Truly spoke," Ben gruffed as he adjusted his gunbelt under a bulging belly. "Them mountains has seen it all, I reckon."

They spoke no more until they rode down Main Street. The town smelled almost new with the scent of freshly cut lumber in some of the buildings, the fresh paint on others, the scent of cherry trees wafting through town from a nearby orchard. The sun was settling behind the mountains, gilding the purple loaves of clouds floating over the snowcapped peaks. Sprays of light etched furrows in the blue sky as majestic and solemn as a stained-glass window in a country church.

Shops were closing up, but John spotted the Platte Hotel down the block and jigged Gent in the flanks with the nubs of his blunt spurs, urging the horse into a lazy lope. Emma and Ben caught up with him.

"I see it," Emma said in a breathy moment of sudden joy. "Oh, Eva, be there."

"Don't get your hopes up, Emma," John said.

"I can't help it. My hopes are up."

"I'm prayin' your daughter's there," Ben said. "Real hard."

"Thank you, Ben," she said, as if to chastise John for his lack of faith.

They stopped in front of the hotel and dismounted. They tied their horses to hitch rings sunk into the ground in front of the new boardwalk. They entered the hotel lobby as a clerk looked up at them from the front desk.

Emma rushed ahead of the two men and clutched the edge of the counter, leaned toward the clerk.

"Do you have a young girl staying here?" she asked. "She'd be with four men."

The clerk, a young man in his twenties, blinked from behind flimsy framed glasses, touched the knot on his string tie and frowned.

"Who's askin'?" the clerk said in his prissiest manner.

"I'm her mother. And those men kidnapped her. Please, tell me where she is."

John stopped beside Emma. Ben braced her on the other side. The clerk stepped backward as if intimidated.

"Why, I'm not sure . . ." the clerk began.

"Answer the lady," John said, hard steel in his voice. "And right quick."

"Yes, sir. They're not here now. Night clerk says they rode out of town early this morning."

"Did they check out?" John asked.

The clerk glanced behind him at the keys hanging on hooks as if that would tell him what he already knew.

"No, sir, they still have their keys and haven't checked out."

"But, you're sure they're not here," John said.

"I'm sure. Yes."

"Give us three rooms. Next to each other. And tell me if you've got a guest named Fergus Blanchett registered."

The clerk ran a finger down the open page of the guest register and shook his head.

"Nope. Nobody here by that name."

"What about those four men and the young girl?"

"See for yourself. The girl was not registered. I don't know what room she was in."

John looked at the names. Brown, Smith, Jones, and Miller.

"Give me the room numbers of those four and put me in a room near theirs." John jabbed a finger into one of the names.

"They are on the first floor and I have only two rooms near them on the same floor."

"Two rooms will do," John said. He felt a gentle kick from the toe of Emma's boot. Ben cleared his throat and rolled his eyes.

"One night or two?" The clerk reached for two sets of keys.

"One night will do," John said.

"That will be four and a half dollars. Two and half for two people in a single room. Please sign the register. Each of you. Separately."

John cast his glance to a nearby bin where there was a stack of newspapers.

"Did you read today's *Rocky Mountain News*?" he asked the clerk.

"I never read that rag."

"Ben, bring one of those papers over, will you?" John said.

Ben walked to the bin and picked up the top paper with

the lurid headlines about the Bobbitt murders. He handed it to John, who placed it upside down on the counter.

"Read that," he said.

The clerk adjusted his eyeglasses, picked up the paper, and read the story about the murders and robberies in Cherry Hill.

"I must say," he said as he put the paper back down. "Are these the people you're looking for, may I ask?"

"The very same," John said.

"Oh, my."

John put a five-dollar bill on the counter. He signed the register, handed the pen to Emma. She signed her name and then Ben scratched something illegible under their signatures.

"Here are your keys. We don't want any trouble here, you understand?"

"You have a sheriff here in town?"

"Yes, we do. Isaac Lucas. His office is just down the street. But he's probably at home or making his rounds at this hour."

"Send somebody to fetch him," John said. "In the meantime, if you see any of these men or that young girl, I want you to come to my room and let me know."

"This is highly irregular, sir. I'm not in the habit of—"

John interrupted him.

"You do that or you're likely to have a lobby full of blood. You savvy?"

"Why, yes. I—I'm going off in an hour or so, but I'll notify the night clerk. You'll be in room 101?"

"And my friend here will be in 102," John said, handing the key to Ben. "You be sure to let me know if any of those men come back here."

"I surely will, sir, and I'll send someone to fetch Sheriff Lucas."

"Make sure of it," John said.

The clerk lifted a bell on the counter and rang it. As John was leading them down the hall to the first floor rooms, he saw a door open and a small man emerged. He was slipping into a black jacket with the name Platte Hotel embroidered in red over his left pocket. He passed them at a trot. John heard the clerk tell him to run over to the sheriff's and have him come to the hotel immediately. As John turned the key in the lock of his room, he saw the man run out the front door.

"Maybe we can even up the odds," Ben said as he walked to the door of 102.

"Maybe we can get that little man to bring us some food," Emma said, a weariness in her voice that softened it almost to a whisper.

Ben unlocked his door. "I'll bring in our rifles and saddlebags," he said. He raised a hand in farewell as John and Emma went inside their room.

"My legs ache," Emma said as she sat on the divan. John lit a lamp on a table in the center of the room. She stretched out her legs and wriggled her toes.

"Nice room," he said.

"The horses are tired and probably hungry," Emma said. "I'm too worn out to take another step."

"We'll take care of the horses after a while. I hope we won't need them tonight."

Emma groaned.

John sat down next to her. He felt the weariness seep through his bones as he extended his legs and relaxed his muscles.

A few moments later, there was a knock on the door.

"I'll get it," John said. He strode to the door and opened it, expecting to see Ben standing there.

Ben was there, but so was the little man wearing the hotel jacket.

"He ain't there," Ben said, "and this man has got some news."

"Step inside," John said to both men.

"I run into a friend of mine on the way over to the sheriff's, Al Moore. He said he was at the Silver Queen this mornin' when Lucas come in and deputized four men and rode out toward Greeley. He ain't been seen since."

"So, no sheriff," John said.

"That ain't all, John," Ben said. He looked at the little man. "You tell him the rest, Mr. Higgins." Ben turned to John. "This is Mortimer Higgins, works here at the hotel."

"What else, Mr. Higgins?" John said.

"Well, sir, Al had just come from the Queen with a snootful, but he said four men and a gal just came into the saloon and took up a table at the back. He said there was talk about the Bobbitt murders, and he and a bunch of others cleared out. He thinks those men might have kilt Lucas and them four who rode out with him."

"Where is this saloon?" John asked.

"Why, it's right down the street. But you better not go there, mister. Al says those men are carrying long guns and packin' iron, and they got a clear view of them batwing doors."

"Thanks, Al."

"What are you aimin' to do, might I ask?"

"I'm not sure, Al," John said, his jawline hardening as his eyes narrowed. "Maybe have a drink at the Silver Queen."

"Lordamighty," Al said. He shook his head as he left the room.

Emma jumped up. "Eva's there with them," she said. "What are we waiting for?"

"I know where the Silver Queen is," Ben said. "I seen its lamps go on when we was outside. It's right in the next block.

"Emma," John said, "you'd better stay here."

"Not on your life, John Savage. I'm going with you."

"I thought you were all tuckered out."

"Not where Eva is concerned. Let's go."

"We walk into that saloon, we're all dead," Ben said, a somber look of defeat in his eyes.

"We're not going to walk into that saloon," John said. "You are."

"Me?"

"I'll tell you all about it on our way over there."

The three left the hotel and walked down the dusty street. There was a pale glow in the sky over the mountains and the bullbats were already winging their way out over the wheat fields and the orchards. There was no traffic on the street.

Longmont looked like a ghost town at that hour, and there was the sense in John's mind of some beast sitting on its haunches, gazing down on them with blazing eyes and a tongue sliding over sharp yellow teeth.

28

LARRY MOON FELT A COLD SHIVER STRIKE BETWEEN HIS
shoulder blades like a splash from a cold bucket of water.
He stifled a gasp and turned to the other bartender who had
arrived a few moments before, Willy Bledsoe.

"That's them, Willy," he whispered. "The ones what was
in the paper this morning."

Willy, a potbellied giant of a man with a fifty-gallon
chest, full black beard streaked with white strands, lollypop-
red cheeks and a moustache dripping over pudgy lips, looked
furtively at the four men and a young girl who had just entered the Silver Queen, the batwing doors still swinging on
their heavy leather hinges. Willy's mouth opened in a sensu-
ous moue, and his sunken blue eyes shimmered with lances
of lamplight.

"Jesus the Christ," Willy murmured. "It is them."

Others in the room looked at the odd queue as Fergus
and the others waded through the maze of tables toward an
empty one in the right-hand corner at the back. Men stopped

dealing cards or held chips in midair as the four men passed them, looking right and left as if they were expecting or welcoming any of the seated men to rise and go for his gun. The room went nearly dead silent as the four men passed, the young girl walking behind the leader as boldly as he.

Then, as Fergus and his gang sat down, moving their chairs so that they were all facing the bar and the door, men got up from their tables, one by one, picking up chips and money, stuffing their pockets as they headed for the ba-twing doors in voiceless retreat. The men at the bar turned to look at the men and the girl seated in the back and exchanged looks. It seemed they had all read the morning paper and had been talking about the Bobbitt murders for much of the day over beers and month-old whiskey made and bottled in Longmont.

"I'll see what they want," Larry said.

"You gonna stay on or go home?" Willy asked as he picked up a fresh towel from beneath the bar and folded it four times.

"I'll stay on, Willy. Either Sheriff Lucas is going to walk in any minute with his deputies and put all those men under arrest, or . . ."

"Or what?"

"Or Lucas and the others are lyin' dead on the post road to Greeley."

"I'd go home if I was you."

"I'm too scared to go home. You stay real close to that scattergun, Willy."

With that, Moon lifted the hinged bar top and walked back to the table, every fiber in his body tingling like a tapped tuning fork.

The colors of the sunset still glowed faintly on the tops of the front windows, and dusk was stealing through the town as more men got up from their tables and walked past the window, all of them turning into shadows that flickered past and disappeared.

"What can I bring you gents?" Moon asked, looking at Fergus, who seemed to be the leader just by his bearing and the way his men surrounded him. The young girl sat between Jubal and Fergus, her face blanched, looking so small and lost, Moon felt a tug at his heart.

"Where are the glitter gals?" Fred asked.

"Too early," Moon said. "The gals will be in later, about an hour after sundown."

"Then, bring us some whiskey," Dick said, "and none of that rotgut made here in town."

"Old Taylor," Fergus said. "Bring us two bottles and four glasses."

"Nothing for the little lady?" Moon said, awonder at his own daring.

"You got any sarsaparilla?" Fergus asked.

"Yep, we do. Fresh made yesterday mornin'."

"Bring her a glass of that," Fergus said.

"Right away," Moon said and strode back to the bar as more men got up and left.

He stood at the bar's service station and gave Willy the order. Willy set out a tray and two bottles of Old Taylor, four heavy glasses. He poured a pale brown liquid into a tall glass for Eva.

"I hope it ain't too fermented," Willy joked.

"I think she's here against her will. Maybe you ought to splash some whiskey in her glass."

"Charge 'em double," Willy said.

"They'll pay when they leave. You charge 'em double, Willy. I'm about to pee my pants as it is."

Willy laughed as Moon picked up the tray and carried it

to the back table. The glasses clinked together because his hands were trembling like the tips of willow branches in a high wind.

Moon set the tray down on the table, then placed the two bottles of whiskey at strategic places, one in front of Fergus, the other in front of Fred. He set empty glasses before each man and placed the glass of sarsaparilla in front of Eva.

"Sorry we don't have no ice," he said to her.

"That's all right," she said in a tiny voice. She drank almost half of it before Moon picked up the empty tray.

"You can pay when you leave," he said to Fergus.

"You send them gals over when they come in," Fred said as he reached for one of the bottles.

"Sure will," Moon said and turned to walk away.

"You and that other barkeep stay where I can see you," Fergus said. "And tell them men still at the bar to stay put."

Moon started to ask why but thought better of it.

"Sure thing," he said and hurried away, leaking urine against his will. It coursed warm and wet down the inside of both legs.

He went behind the bar and whispered Fergus's orders to Willy, who told those few patrons still at the bar that their drinks were on the house while that back table was plumb crowded.

"You mean we can't leave?" asked one man.

"It would be a bad idea," Willy said. "I don't think you'd make it to the door."

"Shit," the man said and glared at the men sitting around the back table.

An hour went by and there was no sign of the women who worked evenings at the Silver Queen. Moon kept glancing anxiously at the doors, but no one came in. And no one left. Finally, one of the men got up from the back table and walked to the bar. It was Fred.

"Where's them gals?" he said to Willy and Larry.

Larry shrugged.

"Damned if I know."

"There better not be anything funny goin' on here," he said.

"They're probably all sick," Willy said. "That sometimes happens."

"Bullshit," Fred said and walked grumpily back to his table.

When the batwings swung open, both Larry and Willy jumped.

They stared at the heavyset man who walked in as if he owned the place.

Ben walked straight to the end of the bar and stood there. He surveyed the empty room and saw the men at the back table. He also saw Eva.

"Sir, you may not want to be here," Moon whispered to Ben.

"Oh, I want to be here, all right. Those are wanted men in the back and that little gal's been kidnapped."

"You ain't meanin' to brace 'em all by yourself?"

"Just bring me a beer and act natural. Will you and the other barkeep back us up?"

"I got a .38 and a scattergun, but I'm so scared I probably couldn't hit the broad side of a barn from six inches away."

"Bring me the beer," Ben said and turned to look at the table.

He raised a hand and waved to Eva.

She bolted upright in her chair and gasped.

Fergus followed her gaze and saw the man standing at

the end of the bar. His eyes narrowed to slits, and he thought hard. He couldn't make out the man's face, nor was there anything familiar about him. But he meant something to Eva.

"Who in hell is that, Eva?" he asked.

She turned to look at Fergus with flashing eyes, a stern expression on her face.

"None of your business," she said.

The night had blackened the front window and devoured the buildings across the street. The barkeep, Larry, brought a glass of beer to Ben and set it before him on the bar.

Ben put two fingers in his mouth and blew a long piercing whistle that startled everyone at the bar and those at the back table.

Then, John and Emma came through the batwing doors as Ben pointed to the back table.

Something invisible sucked all the sound out of the room and replaced it with a heavy foreboding, as if some avenging angel had descended. The lamps flickered but seemed to dim and both barkeeps froze so that they looked like store mannequins behind a pane of glass.

The silence did not last long, but to everyone inside the saloon it seemed an eternity.

29

JOHN AND EMMA EACH GRABBED THE TOP OF A SWINGING DOOR
and pulled it wide open.

A parade of women wearing colorful satin dresses and
black silk stockings paraded through the doors. Each held a
sack. They appeared like a chorus line on stage and lined up
facing the table in the far right corner of the saloon.

Fred and Dick started to rise from their chairs, their
mouths agape.

The girls smiled and upended the sacks. Greenbacks
fluttered from the open sacks and fell to the polished hardwood floors.

"Hey," Jubal yelled, "that's our money." He rose from
his chair as the girls dropped the bags and ran out of the
saloon through the doors still held wide open by John and
Emma.

The men at the bar stared at the money littering the floor,
a look of incredulity on each startled face.

John and Emma let the batwings swing back.

Willy and Larry blinked their eyes in disbelief.

Dick charged toward John and Emma, clawing at his pistol.

Ben stepped away from the bar, pistol in hand, took careful aim, gave the gunman a fair lead and squeezed the trigger.

His pistol belched flame and sparks. The bullet struck Dick in the chest and stopped him in his tracks. The impact hurled the man backward as if he had a rope tied to his back that had suddenly been jerked by an unseen pair of hands.

"Run, Eva, run," Emma shouted as she drew her pistol.

Fred jerked his pistol from his holster and started running toward Emma.

Eva scooted her chair back and dove under a nearby table. Jubal grabbed for her but missed. He drew his pistol.

Fergus upended his table and crouched behind it for protection. He pulled his pistol from its holster and cocked the hammer back.

Emma fired at Fred. Her bullet opened his belly with a tiny hole that spurted blood. He stopped and fired at her. His shot went wild as he struggled to stay on his feet.

Willy raised the double barrels of his shotgun, pulled back both hammers and ticked both triggers. The double-ought buck sprayed Fred with a cloud of lead pellets. He went down like a poleaxed steer, screaming and kicking his legs as blood spewed from a dozen wounds from his neck to his crotch.

Jubal strode toward John, his arm extended, pistol cocked. Before he could fire it, John squeezed his trigger and fired. He fanned the trigger back for another shot as he went into a gunman's crouch. The first bullet smashed into the center of Jubal's chest and he spun around in a dizzy circle. John's second shot ripped into the side of Jubal's head, nicking his ear, exploding one eyeball out of its socket and mashing half of his jaw and all of his nose to bloody rags. Jubal crumpled in a heap, his pistol firing once into the floor, then dropping from his lifeless hand as he crashed to the floor.

"Emma, get behind Ben," John ordered as he wove his way through the room of empty tables, crouched like a panther, zigzagging on the balls of his feet.

Eva began to crawl toward where her mother had gone, scraping her knees on the floor, pushing with her feet to propel herself forward.

Willy reloaded his shotgun with shaking hands. Sweat beaded up on his forehead and drenched his palms as his white shirt dripped and turned dark with perspiration.

Larry brought up his pistol from behind the bar, cocked it, and aimed at the overturned table in the back. There was the sound of splintered wood as the bullet tore through the tabletop and thudded into the wall beyond.

The men at the bar all fell from their stools and flattened against the floor. None of them were armed. A glass of beer overturned and dripped like a miniature amber waterfall onto the brass rail.

Fergus peered around the side of the table and spotted John. He saw Eva crawling toward her mother. His eyes glowed with a malevolent fire as he saw his niece trying to get away.

Ben and Emma both fired at Fergus, who ducked back behind the table. The bullets fried the air over his head, and he emerged on the other side.

John saw a head appear and fired off a quick shot that nipped the edge of the table inches from Fergus's face.

"Lie flat on the floor," John barked to Eva, and she stopped crawling and hugged the floor, her arms and legs sprawled wide. Her eyes filled with tears as she laid her head flat on its side. She trembled with fear, one eye fixed on John, who edged past her, still crouching.

"Give it up, Fergus," John said. "You haven't got a leg to stand on."

"By God, I'll take that little bitch with me," Fergus said. He stood up and aimed his Colt .45 at Eva.

John swung his pistol to bear on Fergus. This took a fraction of a single second. He squeezed the trigger and his gun bucked with the explosion. Fergus looked surprised as John's bullet smashed him just inches from his heart. A terrible pain spread through his chest. His lungs filled with dust before one of them collapsed.

"You . . . you bastard," he growled as he looked at John and tried to bring his arm up to shoot back.

John came within three feet of Fergus, brought his arm up like a flashing scythe, and squeezed off another shot at point-blank range. The bullet plowed a hole through Fergus's forehead and churned his brains to pudding before exploding the back of his skull into dozens of pieces. A rosy spray of blood peppered the back wall as Fergus, his eyes glazed with the final frost of death, half spun as his legs collapsed beneath him. He fell in a distorted heap, his sphincter muscle releasing and seeping a foul stench into the air.

John reached down and lifted Eva to her feet. She embraced him as he holstered his pistol. He put his arms around her.

Emma and Ben ran up to John. Eva looked up and saw her mother. She screamed and dashed into Emma's arms. The two women squeezed each other in a fierce embrace.

Emma looked at John, a grateful expression on her face. Tears rolled down her cheeks.

Her lips moved in a silent phrase that John understood.

"I love you," her lips said.

"I love you, too, Emma," he breathed in a whisper that Eva, Emma, and Ben could hear.

"We got 'em all," Ben said. "My ears are still ringin' from all them gunshots."

Willy and Larry came from behind the bar and looked at the dead men and the piles of money. The men on the floor stood up and stared in abject disbelief at the carnage.

"Let's get out of here," John said, herding his friends toward the door. To the bartenders he said, "That's stolen money, boys. Count it and stack it. Somebody will pick it up."

John, his arm around Emma's waist, Eva's arm around his, walked with Ben out into the cool night air. Silver stars sprinkled light and the Milky Way looked like strewn snow on black velvet.

"That wasn't vengeance," John whispered to himself. "That was justice."

Emma smiled and squeezed his hand. They passed the glitter gals, who emerged from between two buildings.

"Is it over?" one of them asked.

"It's over," John said.

"Plumb over," Ben echoed, and the tittering girls all ran toward the Silver Queen like a bevy of schoolkids responding to the class bell.

John took Emma aside. He gripped her arms with his strong, yet gentle hands.

"What's wrong?" she asked when she saw the intense light in John's eyes as he fixed them on hers.

"I want you and Eva to move back to our ranch, Emma," he said. "We're going to hire more hands and build our herd. I'll pay you more money than you could ever earn in town."

"Doing what?"

"Whatever suits you," he said. "I just want you to have a

home where you both are safe. A town is something to visit, a place to buy goods. I want to give you and Eva a home, a peaceful home in the mountains. A place where you can sit on the porch of an evening and listen to the crickets, the lowing of the cattle, and look at the sky after the sun sets behind those majestic mountains."

"I did find a certain peace up there. Eva and I felt safe."

"Then come back there with me."

"That sounds like a proposition, John."

"Well, it is."

She sighed and gazed into John's eyes with a tender longing.

"Dare I think there could be more to this than just living up there?"

"There could be more, yes."

He filled his lungs with air that swelled his chest. "Much more," he whispered and drew her close to him, wrapped his arms around her holding her tight.

"Oh, yes, John, yes," she murmured, and her words vibrated against his chest and echoed in his heart.